Two Thieves and a Puma

JOHN REESE

DOUBLEDAY & COMPANY, INC.
GARDEN CITY, NEW YORK
1980

All of the characters in this book are fictitious,
and any resemblance to actual persons, living or dead,
is purely coincidental

First Edition
ISBN: 0-385-15372-4
Library of Congress Catalog Card Number 79-7806
Copyright © 1980 by John Reese
All Rights Reserved
Printed in the United States of America

For Nadine and Butch Simas

Two Thieves and a Puma

Chapter One

Broods of quail almost large enough to leave their mothers scattered ahead of the solitary horseman. They were feeding in great flocks among the gooseberry bushes that grew thickly between the live oak trees. A doe with a spring fawn already weaned, but still learning a deer's life from her mother, sprinted gracefully out of sight. An eagle circled tirelessly high overhead, his flight taking him out over the Pacific Ocean, which now and then was visible to the rider. The rattle-brained blackbirds were already succumbing to the hysteria that always preceded the sudden urge to migrate southward.

All this brought peace to the heart of the horseman, but it did not diminish his alertness. His own range, the Flying W, was several miles behind him. He was furtively prowling the land of the Bar H, owned by General Lionel Hethcutt, his brother-in-law. They had not spoken in two years, and even when they met on the street, each looked the other way.

The one tie that could have bound them—Zoe, Alfred Whiting's wife—had been dead for three years. The rift had opened when Sergeant Whiting married Zoe Taorelli; for less than a year earlier, Lieutenant Colonel (and brevet Brigadier General) Lionel Hethcutt, retired, had married Bernardina Taorelli. There was no future in the Army for an enlisted man who was brother-in-law to a rank-conscious martinet like Hethcutt, who forbade his

wife to have anything to do with her sister. She had refused to obey the order—and Hethcutt was not used to
having his orders disobeyed.

There went Sergeant Alfred Whiting's chance of promotion. He had left at the end of his enlistment and had
bought land overlooking the Pacific near Paso Robles,
California. They had one daughter, Bella, who had been
fourteen when her mother died.

Bella now spent most of her time with the Taorelli family in San Francisco, but Bernardina Hethcutt had not left
the ranch the general had bought for two years. They
were not exactly friendly neighbors.

Alf Whiting knew that his own opinion of General
Hethcutt—he insisted on recognition of his brevet rank—
was shared by most of the officers in the Army. He had
heard him described as witless, incompetent, tempera-
mental, starved for praise and recognition. To marry into
the influential Taorelli family had been a form of vindica-
tion for an undistinguished record.

There were also things about General Lionel Hethcutt
that Sergeant Alf Whiting knew personally. He had never
spoken of them to anyone.

Why Hethcutt had bought the ranch adjoining his own
had always puzzled Whiting. Maybe the general was just
trying to prove something to the Taorelli family.

In any case, while the family's status had declined,
Hethcutt's fortunes had prospered. His herds had grown.
He had built a big, new house and other buildings. Meanwhile Alf Whiting still lived in a three-room log cabin,
cooked his own meals except when his daughter came
home or Lon Tsan dropped in. His own herds diminished.
The general had a big crew—Whiting ran his ranch alone.

He suddenly caught a glimpse of white among the
trees. He had been following it for two hours, and now he

had it where he wanted it. He kept himself under total emotional control as he circled and kicked his horse into a canter. In a moment he saw it clearly—a roan and white heifer showing plainly her Shorthorn blood.

He got around her in a ravine and coiled his rope in his hand. She was very heavy with calf, he saw when he got closer. She was springing, which meant that the fetus was so heavy that every step made her external parts bounce. You could figure she would calve within two to four weeks once she started springing.

That was probably why she had left the herd, instinct prompting her to find a good place to bear her calf when the time came. Whiting made his cast when she broke into a clumsy trot just as she cleared the gooseberry bushes.

He caught her around the right hind leg. His horse looked too solidly heavy to be a good cutting horse, but that's what he was. The moment Whiting dallied the rope on the saddle horn the horse turned to face the cow and lean back on the rope, pulling her leg out from under her.

Whiting was out of the saddle at once, carrying a piggin' string—a four-foot strap of rawhide with an eyelet in one end—in one hand. He, like his horse, looked too chunky and strong to be nimble; but nimble he was. He hit the heifer with his shoulder and knocked her down.

Instantly he was on her, looping the piggin' string around one front foot and pulling it back to tie to the free hind foot. Now she was secure. On her hip was the Hethcutt Bar H brand, plainer than her Shorthorn blood.

Only Lionel Hethcutt, damn his soul, had never spent a dime on Shorthorn bulls, while Alf Whiting had sunk the last of his money in a dozen of them. He felt no rage—he was long past that point. All he felt, really, was relief that the heifer was lying quietly, not risking her unborn calf.

But now Whiting worked swiftly, with the skill of long practice. From a gunny sack tied behind his saddle he removed an alcohol-burning blowtorch and a short, miniature branding iron. It had a wooden handle like the top bar of a T. The brand itself was no more than an inch and a half long, and it looked like a simple tally-book check mark.

In three minutes he had the iron just hot enough. He put the check mark on the ground and twisted it to test it. He liked the small wisp of smoke that arose; it would burn a permanent mark but not a deep or painful one.

He ran to the tied heifer and knelt near her hind end. Her udder was already starting to swell. He got his left hand under it and lifted it with a single, powerful muscular spasm.

At the same time he pressed the hot branding iron on the inside of the heifer's leg. She let out one bawl of pain and indignation, and when he let go of her udder, it fell and covered the new brand.

Whiting went back to his horse and put the blowtorch and branding iron down. He returned and expertly removed the piggin' string. He hit the taut rope that connected the cow and the horse, and the horse stepped forward quickly, releasing the strain. He slid the loop off the heifer's foot and stirred her with the toe of his boot.

She got up, a little surprised to find herself free. Whiting smiled to see how well hidden her check-mark brand was. She lumbered off through the oaks and out of sight. As Whiting waited for the branding iron and torch to cool down, he took a small pocket notebook with a heavy leather cover from his shirt pocket.

He turned about halfway through it. He kept his dates secret with a simple pricing code—two words in which no two letters were repeated, each letter representing a number:

PINK   FLOWER
1 2 3 4   5 6 7 8 9 0

Today being October 12, this page was headed PRXPI. He wrote a small, plain hand that anyone could read: "R & W Hfr. abt. IR, spg." That translated into "Roan and white heifer, about twenty months, springing." It was the fifth such notation for today.

He put the notebook back in his pocket and the torch and iron back in the gunny sack. He mounted and turned southward. He had pulled the staples from the fence separating his place from Lionel Hethcutt's and put them in his pocket, merely hanging the wire on the posts. He led his horse through to his own land, dropped the reins so he could feed, and took the fence pliers from the pouch on the saddle.

The pliers were also a hammer. He replaced the wire and hammered in the staples. He mounted and let the reins hang on the horse's neck while he scanned his notebook. Anybody with half good sense could break the code, once he realized that an X meant merely a space. But then what?

The entries covered almost three years. In all that time he had never heard anyone comment on a check-mark brand found on any critter anywhere. But here he had the records showing that 306 head had been so marked, five of them today. And all had displayed good Shorthorn blood.

Only when Alf Whiting had bought those young bulls they were called Durhams. Zoe had been alive then and life had been happy, now and then even gay. Today it was just a disciplined, personal dedication for his daughter's sake. He could daydream without giving way to despair or fury. He could remember the good with pleasure, the bad with anger that never got out of control. That much, at least, he had learned under brevet Brigadier General Lionel Hethcutt.

Durham. What a flood of warm, comforting memories that word brought back! It was when people started calling a Durham a Shorthorn that things had started to go wrong for him. Just coincidence, of course; he did not believe in supernatural omens. But the juncture of events could be credited. Now, of the original twelve Durham bulls he had bought, only four had survived to old age.

He had picked roans and others that were predominantly roan or conspicuously mostly white for a reason. He had known that they all bred back to red eventually, but that two reds could produce a roan, one mostly white, or even a pure white one. He had pored over the figures until he had become sure that the odds were in his favor.

And he could wait. He had waited. But his time of waiting that lay ahead was less than that which lay behind him.

The horse knew it was going home and wanted to run. He held it to a slow canter. Suddenly the horse jumped as a puma screamed from not far away. Cougar, panther, mountain lion—those were all names for the same animal. Whiting still said "puma," the Spanish name, pronounced "pooma."

"Behave yourself, Rance," he said to the horse. "That's just old Sneaky. You know him by now. He won't bother you and I'll probably get a decent meal tonight."

He was then about three miles from home. He heard the puma scream several more times before he reached his place. The trail to it from the Paso Robles road had itself become a road, a shortcut between several places. He begrudged no one the use of his land for this purpose as long as they closed his gates behind themselves, and so far they always had.

There was no smoke coming from the chimney of his log house, which somewhat surprised him. Where the devil was Lon Tsan, usually that most dependable of Chinese? He should have been here yesterday, and he always fixed Whiting a good meal when he visited here.

Whiting kept a milk cow to make cheese, as Zoe had taught him, and she needed feed and milking. He had a dozen horses in the stout corrals that surrounded his house, and they needed water and hay.

I wonder, he thought, where that old booger is. He's overdue, and it's not fair to Sneaky. . . .

He put his horse into a corral and hung saddle and bridle on a pole under a roof. He forked hay to his horses and the cow. He gathered his eggs and carried in firewood, but he did not build a fire. Maybe his luck would still hold and Lon Tsan would show up only a little late.

He did not drink or smoke much, but there was a time and a place for everything. The time was now, when he missed Zoe so piercingly—empty house, cold stove, no kisses, no laughter, no bottom-patting. The place was the bench in the shade on the east side of his house, just outside the kitchen door.

He poured himself a glass of Bourbon, about three ounces, and carried it out and put it on the bench. He took one sip and then began rolling a cigarette. As he tilted his head back to light it, two Chinese came walking around the curve of the road toward his house. They were familiar to him but he did not know their names. He did not want to know.

"Hidy," he said. "He's not here."

One Chinese was very old and gaunt, with papery skin

and curiously blank eyes. The other was young, and while
he was slightly built he conveyed an impression of physical power in his body and in his face one of quick intelli-
gence. It was the young one who answered.

"Him s'pose come today."

"Well, you never can tell about Lon Tsan. Sit down."
He patted the bench. "How about a drink?"

The young man sat down but the old one remained
standing as though hypnotized. The young one shook his
head. "Thank you, but no," he said. "Don't do me no
good, that stuff. But thank you deeply, sir."

The puma made a sort of roaring sound and came into
view down near the corrals. He was an old male, a big
one, but the horses and cattle were used to him. They
went on the alert but they did not panic. The chickens
scattered in all directions for safety, because that was
their natural reaction and not a stupid one. Sneaky had
been known to kill a few chickens. Whiting begrudged
him them but had never taken a shot at him for it.

"That cat," said the young Chinese.

"Yeah, I know. But I don't know if he has spotted Lon
Tsan or only thinks it's time for him."

"I think he know. I think he seen him."

"Could be."

And just then the big cat went bounding up the road
and went out of sight around the curve. Whiting grinned
at the two Chinese, who smiled back.

"Reckon you're right," Whiting said. "It's him."

Both Chinese grinned widely. In a moment, another
Chinese came walking down the road, his shoulders bur-
dened with a light bedroll. He was a powerfully built
man who could have been as young as thirty, as old as
fifty. Like the other two, he had entered the country illegally to work on the railroad. As long as they made no

effort to be conspicuous and worked cheaply, no one paid any attention to them.

"Hidy. You're late," Whiting said, taking another drink.

"Little bit, maybe," said Lon Tsan. "Long walk. Late start. Legs ache sometimes."

He bowed to the other two Chinese, who bowed back. Their eyes glittered with anticipation.

"You going to feed me first?" Whiting asked.

"I start the fire, Alf, and while the stove heat up, I take these gen'men downstairs, all right?"

"Fine with me."

Lon Tsan went into the kitchen and began building a fire in the cookstove. The puma had lain down and stretched out no more than twenty feet away. When Lon Tsan came to the door to motion to the other Chinese, the cat got up and streaked toward the door.

Lon Tsan put his foot out and shoved the cat's big head aside with his foot. "You be good!" he said. "Not time yet."

He nodded. The other two Chinese went inside. Whiting, sipping his whiskey, heard the cellar door lifted with a screech of heavy hinges. The cat shot through the door and down the dark steps, but Lon Tsan took time to light a lantern before leading the two Chinese down to the earth-walled cellar.

Whiting finished the whiskey and got up to stoke the fire. Perhaps half an hour passed before Lon Tsan came up the steps alone.

"What you got to cook a dinner with?" he asked. Like the younger of the other two Chinese, he had no trouble pronouncing his *r*'s.

"Killed a steer the other day and sold off most of it, but I saved a whole loin because I figured it was about time for you to show up. How about some steaks tonight and you put the rest of that loin in the oven to roast?"

"Sure. Got any spuds?"

"Plenty of spuds, plenty of onions. How about some sliced raw onions with steak and fried spuds?"

"Sure!"

"Your friends all right?"

"For now. Have to go see them again in a minute. Old man, he need too much. Old man like him get his ass in a jam and mine too someday."

"Don't get mine in one."

Lon Tsan shook his head. "I would never do that." He tapped his head with his forefinger. "I have just ordinary sense, but I stop to think. I am never rash. And I do not want to get rich—only to help a few friends."

"Like Sneaky."

The Chinese smiled and nodded as he went efficiently ahead with his cooking.

Sneaky was—let's see, now—almost seven years old. Whiting had staked out a calf pen where a puma had already killed and carried away two very young calves, and had shot her in the act of taking a third one. She was only badly wounded, and he was able to track her when daylight came. He found her dead near her den, with her two kittens whimpering lonesomely beside her.

He had put both kittens in a bag and taken them home for Zoe to raise. The female did not survive, but the male became a pet and a pest. He grew large for a puma, and he loved to try to get up into Zoe's lap and be cuddled. When she died he was disconsolate and, at times, savage.

Lon Tsan turned up about then. He had a beat that he walked from San Francisco to south of San Luis Obispo, selling opium to a few scattered Chinese smokers who did not have access to a commercial smoking house. There were then five such men in this area, one of them being General Hethcutt's cook. It amused Whiting to let Lon Tsan use his cellar as an opium den with Hethcutt's cook as a client.

Now there were only three clients, and only the old man who had arrived today was heavily addicted. Whiting had tried it once, but it frightened him and he never again risked addiction. Lon Tsan, of course, was less seriously addicted, and only through attending his clients and spending so much time in a closed room full of opium smoke.

The same thing had happened to Sneaky, the puma. He had always enjoyed the cellar, and there had been no keeping him out when Lon Tsan's customers were there. For a few days after "having his pipe," Sneaky was loving and lovable. Then he became solitary and a little cranky. By the time Lon Tsan was due again, he was downright disagreeable.

Whiting took no pay from anyone for playing host to Lon Tsan, but he knew if he ever needed money, the Chinese would get it for him. Whiting did not approve of opium smoking or opium eating, but people did it everywhere, and he kept some around for medicinal purposes. As a painkiller, or for curing diarrhea, it had no substitute.

Two doctors relied on Whiting to keep them supplied, and Lon Tsan's was a high-grade product. It was not a business Whiting would have sought out, but he liked the Chinese and enjoyed their long talks. And having quick money available on a friendly loan was an advantage not to be sneezed at.

In a strange way he felt at home with Lon Tsan—strange, because of his marriage to Zoe. In their loyalty to family, the Chinese and Italians were much alike. Alf had

no idea what Lon Tsan's real business was. The opium
was plainly both a sideline and a subterfuge of some kind.
But he liked the man, and behind Lon Tsan he sensed the
organized power of one of the big and influential Chinese
families.

The two ate late, while downstairs in the cellar, two
Chinese and a big, happy puma enjoyed the solace of the
"heavenly flower." Before daylight, Lon Tsan would hitch
up a team of Whiting's horses to a light wagon and
deliver his two clients to wherever they worked. Whiting
did not know where it was, and he did not want to know.
And sometime later, Sneaky would come carefully up the
steep cellar steps and slouch outside, stopping halfway to
the barn to relieve himself.

Whiting would close the cellar door in the floor of the
kitchen and Sneaky would slip off somewhere to sleep it
off in some favorite hiding place. Whiting would go on
about his work, and when he returned in the afternoon he
would find his team and wagon in place, dinner on the
stove waiting to be heated up, and Lon Tsan gone until
next week.

Lon Tsan had done the dishes and made the whole
house spotless—which was why Alf Whiting had the reputation of being such a persnickety-clean bachelor. The
one thing Lon Tsan could never learn to do was roll a cigarette. When he had finished his work, Whiting got out
the makin's and rolled two cigarettes.

"I'm kind of tired tonight, Lon Tsan," he said. "I'll
smoke this and turn in. Somehow I'm not in the mood to
talk tonight."

"Has General Hethcutt made trouble for you?" the
Chinese asked.

"No. I'm making some for him but it can't be for a
while yet, and I get impatient waiting."

"You must not do that. I wanted to tell you that I saw your very beautiful daughter on Sunday."

"The hell you did!"

"Oh, yes. She was going to church with her cousins. She was wearing a blue dress with a darker blue sash, a white cape, and a white hat. She is very beautiful, and I think very good."

"I don't know when I'll get to see her again." Whiting gritted his teeth. "When her aunt finally gets her gall up, she'll make Hethcutt ask her down for a visit. Then she'll be able to ride over and see me a couple of times. I don't know when I'll ever get to San Francisco to see her. The Taorellis don't exactly welcome me, either."

Lon Tsan touched Whiting's arm delicately. "I walked behind them for three blocks. Nobody pays any attention to a humble Chinese in San Francisco. I heard her talking. She is very lonely to see you. She is very proud of her father, and she wishes she could come here and live with you. I hope that makes life happier for you."

It was a long time before Whiting said, "It don't. God, I'm going under fast here! I can't bring her down here to this—this boar's nest, when I can't even be sure I'm going to be able to keep it."

"You are not giving up, are you?"

"No, but I need another year. Maybe even then I won't be able to save my place. Every year my calf crop gets smaller, and I know why. If I can raise the money to hire a good lawyer a year from now, I've got a chance."

"You don't want to talk about it any more?"

Whiting shook his head. "Not now. It's too risky."

"When you are ready, I know the man you must talk to. He is not a lawyer but he is a very good man, very smart, very brave. My family had some bad things happen in San Francisco and he brought them justice. And he only charges what you can afford—big fees to rich people, small fees to poor."

"Who is he?"

"A private detective, Mr. Jefferson Hewitt, of Bankers Bonding and Indemnity Company, of Cheyenne, Wyoming. Here is his card. Do not wait too long, old friend, before you call on him. I think if you tell him you were a simple soldier and that an officer is robbing you, it may make a difference. He was a simple soldier too, at one time."

Whiting took the card without enthusiasm, but he put it in his wallet rather than offend Lon Tsan. Lon Tsan went on to tell him how a cartage company had forged some bills for services never rendered to his family's companies and won a lawsuit in court that would have cleaned Lon Tsan's family out. Jefferson Hewitt had secured the information that enabled a lawyer to win a reversal of the case, and had even found a bank that would lend the family money to keep going until the case could be settled.

"I don't know as he'd want to mix up in a case where there wasn't much money involved and there was a chance he'd be killed. Hethcutt has got the damndest bunch of brutes working for him now. He terrorizes people, that's what he does."

"He won't terrorize Mr. Hewitt. You have my word on that."

"I'm still not ready, though."

"Let me know when you are, friend. I'll send him a telegram to come to San Francisco. He will come if I call."

Somehow Whiting felt better. "Let me think about it, but I've still got to have a little time. Listen, do you know anything about a fellow they call Crazy Ozzie Hyde?"

"Only what I hear, but what I hear I can believe.

Crazy Ozzie Hyde is a very bad man. He kills people for pleasure and he is very good with a gun. The last I heard, he was working as a deputy sheriff to kill a very bad robber, I think in Amador County."

"Well, he's working for Lionel Hethcutt now."

"Amazing! Doing what?"

"Supposed to be a cowhand."

"Do not believe that. This man is a killer. But he is not as dangerous as Mr. Jefferson Hewitt. Mr. Hewitt is the fastest and straightest shot in the world."

For a moment, Whiting's ordinarily impassive face went red with suppressed fury. It was only a second or two before he controlled it.

"It's not time yet, Lon Tsan. I have to wait awhile, and I can wait as long as necessary. I have already waited two and a half years."

"You have the patient stamina of a Chinese, my friend. But when the time comes, remember this man."

"I'll remember him." Whiting waited a moment and then smiled his stiff but still warm smile at Lon Tsan. "When the time comes, that is."

Chapter Two

About a year and a half later—in late April, to be exact—a
southbound Southern Pacific train that had left Paso
Robles only a quarter of an hour earlier began to slow
down for a flag stop that was rarely used. There were
holding pens for up to one thousand cattle, three loading
chutes, and an untidy roofed building with wide eaves
and a brick floor that served as a waiting room for the
rare passengers that arrived or departed here.

It was a mixed train, with a baggage and mail car, a
passenger car, three box cars, and five slatted livestock
cars. The conductor, in his blue uniform, entered the passenger car and went down the aisle to where a man and
a girl sat together.

"Be there in about two minutes," he said to the man. "I
want to drop off these stock cars on the passing track, so
we'll pull straight into it and uncouple them. That'll put
you on the wrong side of the depot, but there's not much
difference, sir."

"What are you going to do with your caboose—just
leave it here?" the passenger asked.

"Oh, no. We'll pull out on the main line and back up
and put it on in front of the engine. Real bad grade coming up, and it's easier to push than pull. I hope it's all right
if you get off on the wrong side."

"Fine with me. This is beautiful country and you keep
a clean passenger car. I hate to leave you, frankly."

"Why, thank you very much, Mr. Hewitt. Not many people notice things like that."

"They don't ride the rails as much as I do, either," said Jefferson Hewitt. "No telegrapher here, I suppose?"

"No, sir."

The train clanked to a stop while the front-end brakeman opened the switch to the passing track. They started up again, clacking across the switch points and rocking gently on the inferior, little-used roadbed. Looking past the girl and out of the window, Hewitt saw several pens full of fat cattle, and three men on horseback.

The train stopped once more to detach the livestock cars. The conductor opened the door on the left-hand side of the front of the car, folded up and locked the hinged platform, and descended the three iron steps it had concealed carrying his detraining stool. He put it on the ground and waited while Hewitt and the girl came down the aisle and descended the steps.

Hewitt offered his hand. "I like to know the name of the man who has been such a good host. You already know mine," he said.

"I'm Abe Miller. Thanks for your kind words," the conductor said, gratefully. "I was told to take good care of you by Milt Sydney. I guess you know him."

"I know he's your chief of protection and investigation, that's all, but I know a dick on the Santa Fe who put in a good word for me. Thank you again."

The girl offered her hand, too. "Thank you, sir. It has been a pleasure to travel with you."

"Why, gee whiz, that's surely nice of you."

The conductor mounted the steps with his stool, dropped the platform, and closed the door. The train, minus the stock cars and the caboose, pulled on through until it had cleared the switch at the south end of the passing track. It began backing down on the other side of the station so it could pull in and take the caboose on the front of the engine before backing out on the main line again.

One of the three horsemen hastily dismounted and came hurrying toward them. He was gray-haired, with a solid, healthy body and an unlined but solemn face. The girl ran to him, leaving her big valise, and threw herself into his arms.

"Oh, Dad, oh, Dad, I hope you're not going to be angry with me, but if you're having trouble with Uncle Lionel, I want to be with you," she said.

"He's not going to take it very kindly, and neither is your Aunt Bernardina," the man said.

"I don't care. Grandma had a fit, but I told her this is where I belong. She said she'd have to think it over very carefully before taking me back to finish school, but I don't even care about that."

The man cupped his daughter's shining face in his hands and kissed her gently on the forehead. She was a pretty girl, with the mass of black curls of her Italian mother, and blue eyes that could have come from her father or a blond Lombard strain—or from both. Now, with her fair face flushed with emotion and her eyes glinting with unshed tears, she was downright beautiful.

Alf Whiting looking over her shoulder and said, "You'd be Mr. Hewitt, I reckon."

"That's right, and you'll be Alfred Whiting."

"Yes, sir. You kind of knocked the wind out of me, bringing my daughter along."

"I didn't bring her. She came."

"How'd you two get together?" There was a slightly suspicious tone in Whiting's voice.

"My clumsiness, and worse clumsiness on the part of

an undiplomatic banker. My firm bonds the staff of the Tuscan-American National Bank. I wanted to learn all I could about this situation before I came here, and I was talking to the bank president when he suddenly blurted out, 'Why, here's one of the Taorellis now, Miss Whiting!'"

"And before I gave up I had pumped him dry, Dad," the girl said.

"Not quite," said Hewitt, as he and Whiting shook hands. "There's a lot I need to know before I even decide if we can accommodate you, but we can talk later."

"This evening. I'm not going to try to load these critters until the northbound freight gets in, and God knows when that will be."

"It was running on time, according to the train orders our conductor got in Paso Robles."

"I'll still wait. They'd wait for General Hethcutt, and by God, they'll wait for me, too." He waved to his two men to come to the tiny station. "We're fixed up with a bait of grub because you never can tell when you're going to get home, these days. Let's eat. Now, I don't have any regular help, Mr. Hewitt. These are just a couple of fellows I picked up for a week, so be careful not to talk in front of them."

There was a covered pail of coffee that they heated over a wood fire. There were big slabs of tender beef, broiled black on the outside and left juicy and red inside. There was a pan of corn bread.

The two men who worked for Whiting today were silent, a little shy around his daughter. One was an old rider who had probably worked cattle from Saskatchewan to Sonora and had never had ten dollars to spare in his life. The other was a big brute of a man whom Whiting called "Hippo." He had taken a bad beating recently, and it would be another week or two before his face healed.

As they ate, they talked. "I've got a hundred and thirteen prime head going out today, and that's my crop for two years," Whiting said. "I left myself eighty breeding cows and heifers and my five best young bulls. I was better off five years ago, when I was just another raggedy-pants cowman with big idees."

For the first time, Hippo spoke in a hoarse and gravelly voice. "Your neighbor, old Hethcutt, he's done all right."

"Yes, he has," Whiting said, carefully. "Yes sir, he sure has."

"Understand he's a relation of yourn."

"By marriage only, Hippo."

Hippo stopped chewing to swallow a chunk of beef. Then he said, "I'll tell you one thing, Mr. Whiting. He's got a man working for him that I'll shoot on sight—in the back if I can. Maybe you know him. They call him Crazy Ozzie. I don't know his last name."

"It's Hyde," said Whiting.

Hippo said nothing more, but his fingertips went up to touch a long scab that began at the left corner of his mouth and trailed halfway across his cheek. Hewitt studied the man a minute.

"Got the bead on you and then pistol-whipped you, did he?" he said.

Hippo's small eyes narrowed. He nodded but did not speak. Hewitt poured himself a cup of coffee but handed it to Bella Whiting to drink first.

"You don't want to shoot him in the back, Hippo," he said. "Take his gun away from him and break him in two with your bare hands."

"You don't know him. This fella is a real gunslinger."

"I would beat him to the draw without getting to my feet, my friend. No matter how good these bad boys think they are, there's always somebody better, and usually it's me."

He wore gray woolen pants stuffed into fine boots, a white shirt with a silk scarf instead of a tie, and a black hat creased like a cavalryman's. His tailored black jacket was buttoned by only one of its buttons.

When Bella started to hand him the cup of coffee, he made as if to reach for it. Instead his hand slid inside the coat and came out with a .45 that had lain in a holster of his own design that clipped to the belt that held up his trousers. It was held in place by a spring-loaded pawl that closed on the front sight, but a simple twist in drawing it made the gun fall into his hand.

He cocked it as he drew. He snapped a quick shot at one of the green glass insulators on the pole that carried the telegraph line. He did not shatter it, but he nicked it. He put the gun back in its holster and took the coffee cup.

After a moment of stunned silence, Hippo said, "That's mighty fine shooting or mighty lucky shooting."

Sometimes one small demonstration saved thousands of words. He liked big Hippo, and now he had him on his side. He had startled Alf Whiting, too, and he was a hard man to startle.

"If you're a good shot you get luck, too, more often than not," Hewitt said, smiling.

Hippo squinted thoughtfully. "You mebbe would kill Crazy Ozzie."

"I've heard you're a trick shot," said Whiting.

"Oh, in a way, perhaps," said Hewitt. "I'll tell you a little secret. I learned to shoot a forty-five in the Army. I learned to shoot it accurately at its maximum range. I stay in practice, getting the gun out and firing at a distant and difficult target like that insulator. Your quick-draw artist has to get in close because he can't spare the time to aim. I just see to it that he never gets that close."

"Why would Uncle Lionel keep a crazy gunman on his crew, Dad?" Bella Whiting asked her father.

"That's just one of the questions I can't answer and won't even try," Whiting said. He cocked his head and listened a moment and then went on, "I hear her blowing. Let's stomp this fire out and get these critters loaded."

The train shortly appeared, coming from the south. It stopped, detached the engine and a couple of cars, and went on down to the switch to back in on the passing track. Hewitt found Bella a place where she could watch safely on top of the plank fence.

They loaded the four cars quickly. The train pulled out. Whiting took out a deep leather purse and paid off the two men. The older one accepted it meekly but in silence. "Tell you the truth," Hippo said, as he took his, "I figgered you and me was going to have trouble. Two dollars a day is what you promised, but there's always *de-ducts* most of the time."

Whiting grinned. "Nope. I can't ask a man to stay for only five days' work for less than two bucks a day."

"You got a steady man?"

"No."

"You need one."

"But I can't afford one, Hippo. And I couldn't pay any two dollars a day steady."

"I'll work for you for a dollar a day and wait until you can pay me."

"Why?"

"Because there's something going on here that I can't figure out. Something tells me Crazy Ozzie is part of it. I'd like to be around when him and Mr. Hewitt butt heads."

Whiting thought about it. "Come see me day after tomorrow. Mr. Hewitt and I have some thinking and talking to do."

He shook hands with both men and watched them ride off. Hewitt took both valises, his and Bella's, on behind his saddle. The girl got up and sat sidewise behind her father. The horse did not like it but both Whiting and the girl looked to be at home on him.

It was a slow ride of nearly three hours before Whiting's place came into view. There was little talk, but at the first sight of her home, Bella gave a cry of delight.

"Oh, there's old Sneaky! Does Lon Tsan still come around?"

Whiting looked embarrassed. "Yes, and that's something I got to explain to Mr. Hewitt when we can be alone. Lon's due in tomorrow or the next day, and Sneaky's kind of cranky now. Don't try to pet him and don't let him into the house."

Sneaky, it seemed to Hewitt, was a huge male puma that seemed to have the run of the place. He would weigh better than one hundred and fifty pounds, and was in perfect condition. He came loping to meet them, smelled a stranger, and turned and vanished into the live oak timber that surrounded the place.

"I'll find something to cook for supper, Dad. You and Mr. Hewitt have your talk," Bella said.

The two men sat on the woodpile in the sun. The hills were green now under the trees, but the winter rains were over and soon all this range would wear its summer brown. The trees would remain green, but it would be a dusty, darker green as they struggled to survive on the water they had hoarded in their root systems and that which remained in the subsoil.

"Beautiful country," Hewitt said. "How far is it to the ocean from here?"

"Say six miles. I usually have a little drink before supper. Can I offer you one? Bourbon's all I've got, but it's good stuff."

"Bourbon is my drink."

Whiting brought out his bottle and two glasses and poured two stiff drinks. Inside the house, Bella sang as she worked in the kitchen. Haltingly, Whiting told Hewitt about Lon Tsan and his opium traffic. Hewitt laughed until tears came to his eyes.

"An opium-smoking puma! I've tried it but I think the traffic should be suppressed. It's a bad business, Mr. Whiting, but we all make our little compromises with life and I've found that the Chinese are good friends to have. It's a hell of a trick to play on the cat, though."

Sneaky appeared several times as they talked. Each time he seemed to decide not to trust this stranger in the white shirt.

"I know I've been missing cattle year after year, and I know where they've gone," Whiting finished his story by saying. "It's hard to believe a man could be such a thieving son of a bitch, but you don't know General Hethcutt."

"I've heard of him. I did my hitch in the Army myself, and I keep track of things. How many head do you reckon he has taken from you?"

"Has to be close to two thousand by now."

Hewitt whistled. "What is it you expect of me?"

"After supper I want to show you something, and then you tell me what to do with it."

Supper was a gay affair. Whiting was deeply moved to have his daughter at home again, and she was delighted to be there. Hewitt was not quite sure what she expected of him. She had been sedate enough on the train, but now she was pretending a warmer relationship than really existed. She patted his arm now and then, leaned across the table to press her big, handsome bust against the table and make it more prominent, and suddenly was calling him "Jeff."

Not twenty-one, and convent-educated, he decided, and just practicing her flirting on a man old enough to make it a safe pastime. On the other hand, she had a poise that seemed to make practice a waste of time.

While she was washing the dishes, Whiting lighted a lantern and led the way out to the shop that was attached to his small hay barn. From a pile of nondescript junk in the corner he dragged a gunny sack, and from it he took an alcohol blowtorch and a short branding iron with a hickory handle, an iron that made a check mark only about an inch and a half long.

"I brought the first Shorthorn blood into this country—only it was called Durham then," Whiting said. "That son of a bitch of a Hethcutt never owned anything but culls and half-blood Galloways, but the last few years he has been shipping beef that is plainly Shorthorn. Now, where the hell did that blood come from?

"There's a three-wire fence between us. He's got the manpower to keep it up, but no three-wire is going to hold a bull that wants to get to a cow in heat. I brought most of those bulls in to sell. I sold one, just one, and I didn't get the others branded in time. Funny thing, a few months later I saw two or three good Shorthorn bulls wearing the Bar H brand.

"What was I going to do, raise a family stink and accuse my own brother-in-law when my wife was dying? When every cent I had was going on doctor bills and he was keeping a dozen men to do the work six could do?

The overbearing bastard just looked me in the eye and stole me blind."

"Pulled rank," said Hewitt.

"That's exactly it, and I had to let him get away with it because of my wife. After she was dead it was too late. At least Hethcutt thought so."

Whiting picked up the branding iron. "I was down to breeding stock I had to have if I was going to stay in business. I had nothing left to sell—nothing! I rode fence line and tried to keep the fences in repair. Every now and then, I'd see a young heifer with my brand on her. You ever try to brand a calf crop by yourself? I got maybe twenty, thirty, branded.

"Then I worked this thing out where I could brand a calf by myself where it wouldn't show. I've branded over four hundred and twenty head—a hell of a lot more than I've owned and sold in these years. I want you to back me up when I file a lawsuit and claim a thousand head of good grade Shorthorns of his."

"I don't know what I could do," Hewitt said, puffing thoughtfully at his cigar. "What you need is a good lawyer."

"And somebody with the guts to face Hethcutt down when the lawyer tells him about this secret brand. I can't do it by myself. You're an expert on cattle cases. You worked other rustling cases, haven't you?"

"Yes. Mr. Whiting, you've got a damned ingenious idea here, but it seems to me that cashing in on it could be a problem. Let me think it over."

Whiting's shoulders slumped. He cocked his ear to listen to his daughter's singing in the kitchen. His whole world was wrapped up in her, that was plain.

His eyes came around to meet Hewitt's. "Mr. Hewitt,

so help me God, you're my last hope on earth," he burst
out, hoarsely.

———— ◄ ◆ ►———

There were two bedrooms in the cabin. Whiting gave
up the big one to his daughter and offered the small one
to Hewitt, who rejected it with a smile and a firm shake
of his head. Whiting said that when he had men working
for him, they slept in the hay barn and ate in the kitchen.

"The hay barn suits me fine," Hewitt said.

"All right, but there's no way to keep that damned
puma out of it," said Whiting. "Just don't do anything to
scare him or make him mad and you'll be all right."

"I'm pretty tired. He could get right in bed with me
and I wouldn't know it."

Which was almost what happened. The lion came into
the hay barn several times as Hewitt lay awake, thinking
over this strange situation. His emotions told him to take
the case, for several reasons.

The first was that, as an enlisted man himself, he had a
natural sympathy for any other enlisted man who was
being bullied by an officer. He had picked up what information he could about Hethcutt around San Francisco,
and what he had heard made the general an easy man to
dislike. In his long career as a detective, he had met many
a general who could lead and command without being
pompous and overbearing. The temptation to take this
one down a notch was strong.

He liked Alf Whiting. A plain man, but by no means
stupid. He had not thought through his plan to recover
what was his by the branding iron that made a hidden
check mark, but it was ingenious if a lawyer could figure
out how to use it.

Then there was the girl, whom he could see clearly in

the dark, to his annoyance. He liked women but he was
not a marrying man, and to get mixed up with one as
young as Bella—oh no, oh no!

Crazy Ozzie Hyde was a factor, too. Hewitt detested
the madmen who called themselves "gunslingers" with
such bullying, menacing, vicious braggadocio. He had
never yet met one who had all his buckles buckled, and
this one already had the nickname "Crazy." It would be
nice to make a nice boy of him.

The truth was, Hewitt had not been quite candid with
Whiting. He was on a far more important case for an Italian banker in San Francisco, and Alf Whiting's connection with the Taorelli family had happened to come up
only in his discussions there. Too much money was involved in the bank case for him to get involved in cattle
rustling. But if Alf Whiting's problem could give him an
opening wedge into his real job, it was a piece of luck.
And Hewitt had learned to believe he was a lucky man,
most of the time.

Jefferson Hewitt had come out of the Ozarks so young
that he had to lie about his age to enlist in the Army at
the Presidio of San Francisco. He could read and write,
that was about all. He had no ambition to become an
officer, especially after he saw what power and freedom a
company clerk had.

He tried to make himself the best company clerk in the
Army, and some officers swore he was. He learned gram-
mar by reading and studying. He read a book a day, or
more. He let learning become an addiction, like smoking
opium. He was not a man of genius but he had his talents,
and he had honed them to the utmost.

He spoke fluent Spanish, pretty good German and
French, and enough Italian to get by. He was an excellent
portraitist with professional crayons and he thought he

might have been a real artist. He studied all forms of gambling until he could have made his living at cards.

He was an expert masseur and could have made a living at that, too. He was a wood-carver, handy with all tools. He was an excellent horseman and a good judge of all livestock.

His partner in Bankers Bonding and Indemnity Company was Conrad Meuse, a German who had taught philosophy in the old country but who had also learned accountancy. Both men were loners, both loved a good fight, both liked to win—and both liked money. Conrad invested Hewitt's money as he did his own. Hewitt was a rich man, at home in the dining rooms and theaters of the sophisticated East. But he could also go without bathing or shaving and wear rags, if that was what it took to get him to the heart of a case.

His marksmanship with either long or short gun was a legend. No man was that good, but Hewitt cherished his reputation because it made many a gunfight unnecessary. His favorite weapon was a limber, leather, shot-filled sap, which he used with surgical precision.

Conrad was convinced that Hewitt was a tomcat who spent most of his time passionately pursuing females. Hewitt smiled in the dark as he wondered what Conrad would think if he could see Bella Whiting, and if he knew the many, many opportunities there would be to be alone with her on this tree-dotted Pacific littoral.

What probably made up his mind, after he had dozed off undecided, was Sneaky.

Hewitt came awake suddenly, feeling a warm body stretched out close to his and hearing a deep, rasping breath in his very ear. He was about to leap up, shouting, and try to get his hands on his .45 when he remembered the opium-smoking puma. Purring, that was what he was doing—purring like a house cat!

I suppose I should be flattered that he likes me, Hewitt told himself, but he picked a hell of a time to demonstrate it. . . . The big cat knew he was awake now, and snuggled still closer. If he could not have his pipe, human companionship was at least a form of solace.

All night—or what remained of it—they slept side by side. Once Hewitt dozed off and woke up with his arm across Sneaky. Cautiously he removed it. Sneaky squirmed a little and kept squirming until Hewitt put the arm back.

What would Conrad Meuse say if he knew who his bedmate was tonight? All right, Hewitt thought, I'll have a go at it. I've got to see how this turns out. . . .

"Shut up and go to sleep!" he said, peevishly. The sound of a human voice seemed to be what Sneaky was waiting for. He lay still and slept.

Chapter Three

Keeping under cover of the trees as much as possible, they rode to the ridgetop from which the valley to the east was visible. Hippo pointed to a spot halfway down the slope.

"Right there is where it is, only you can't see it because the slope falls off pretty steep there. But that's General Hethcutt's place. He runs it like an army camp. Good bunkhouse but rotten grub. Docks your pay when he figgers you dogged it on something, and you yessir him and like it," he said.

"How many men does he work?" Hewitt asked.

"I hear twelve right now, not counting the cook. But make that eleven. Crazy Ozzie Hyde ain't a man. He's some kind of an animal."

"Hippo, you can't let something like that fester in your mind. I know you're not afraid of him, but believe me, you will be if you don't stop thinking about him. You'll be less a man than you are now."

Hippo said nothing. He had been working for Alf Whiting for ten days now, and his wounds had all healed on the outside. The beating he had taken had embittered him so deeply, however, that Hewitt worried about his mental stability.

The two bunked in a little room partitioned off in the corner of the hay barn. There was always an unwritten rule against smoking around hay storage, but Hippo had scraped the floor down to the dirt and smoked all the time in the bunkroom. In the middle of the night, Hewitt would awaken and see the glow of the big man's cigarette, as he sat on the edge of his bunk in his underwear— thinking, thinking, thinking.

He was an odd one, this Hippo Thompson. He was neither alarmed nor amused by Sneaky. When Lon Tsan's visits here were explained to him, he merely nodded. Hewitt had told him of his own job here, and all Hippo had said was "Good! Time somebody fought that old son of a bitch back."

"Remember," Hewitt had said, "it's Hethcutt I'm trying to get a bead on, not Crazy Ozzie."

"I know. You got your job and I got mine."

No use trying to talk to him. Several times, Hippo had told him about his trouble with Crazy Ozzie. Hippo had approached General Hethcutt and his crew in Three Oaks, the little town on the stage road south of Paso Robles, to ask for a job.

"Not hiring," the general had said, not even turning his head to look at Hippo.

Hippo followed him. "I hear you're getting ready to break a string of horses for the market. I'm as good a horsebreaker as there is in the world. Just give me a chance to prove it, mister."

He had not known then that it was an offense against Hethcutt's dignity to be addressed as "mister" instead of "General." Hethcutt was a man a little below average height, with a heavy mane of white hair that he grew long, and a big, white mustache. His eyes were small, and they glittered like blue glass marbles under shaggy white brows. He walked erectly, pacing with a somewhat stiffkneed, arrogant gait, looking neither to the left nor right.

Without looking around, he said, "Ozzie, get rid of this man for me."

A lean and slightly humpbacked man whose grizzled whiskers had not been shaved in two weeks got in front of Hippo. About six feet separated them then. The general had already walked on.

"Don't take a step closer," Crazy Ozzie said.

"Get out of my way," said Hippo. "That man is going to give me a civil answer or—"

"You son of a bitch!"

It was said deliberately, to make Hippo go for his gun. He had never claimed to be much of a hand with a .45, but there were some things a man couldn't take in front of others, and the whole Bar H crew was standing there grinning. Hippo started awkwardly to take out his gun.

Crazy Ozzie Hyde's .45 seemed to jump into his hand. It was pointed steadily at Hippo's guts from less than six feet away before Hippo had a good grip on his own. Crazy Ozzie let him size up the situation a second or two.

Then he said, "When I tell you something, I expect you to listen. I guarantee next time you will." He walked toward Hippo, gun in hand. Suddenly he raised it and slashed at Hippo's face with the muzzle. Hippo, startled, leaped back and yelled. The barrel of the gun caught him on the cheek rather than the forehead, but then Ozzie brought the butt down on the top of Hippo's head and dropped him to his knees.

He pounded him methodically with the side of the gun until Hippo fell, unconscious. He was sure he had been hit eight or ten times. When he came to, he had several deep, bruised cuts on his face that were bleeding badly.

The doctor who stitched them up, and then charged him only one dollar when he learned that Hippo had only two, said that Hippo had asked for it. "That's why he's called 'Crazy,' because he is. Kill-crazy. I take care of the general's family and crew but I already told him that Hyde could lay there and bleed to death and I wouldn't lift a hand."

"What did the general say to that?" Hippo asked.

"I'll never forget it. He just smiled and said, 'That's his problem, not mine. I run my business my way and you run yours to suit yourself.'"

When Hewitt had heard the story for the third or fourth time, he told Hippo not to mention it again. "It sounds to me like General Hethcutt is the crazy one, Hippo," he said. "I mean that! Power does that to some people. Combine it with greed, with fear of running out of money, or whatever else is eating on him, and he could have jumped the rails."

Now he turned his horse and, with Hippo following, headed back for Alf Whiting's place. Hethcutt ran around four thousand head of cattle. Raised horses that he sold to Army Remount and had a hundred or more culls to auction off every year.

From Whiting he had learned that the Taorellis had turned over ten thousand dollars when the general retired to go into the cattle business. Part of it was a gift, their daughter's own money, the rest a loan. Couple of years ago, Hethcutt had settled the loan by selling his wife's family a 15 per cent interest in the Bar H and all the livestock on it.

Whiting himself had received five thousand from his wife's family, but Zoe had had to create a scene to get it. It was her own money, inherited from a maternal aunt. Her will left it to Whiting and, if he died before her, to their daughter.

The Taorellis were not big businessmen, but there were a lot of them and they were fishermen, merchants, com-

modity brokers—anything that made money. "They're
nice folks," Alf said, "but too damn impressed with a
brevet brigadier's star. Now that there's bad blood between him and me, I don't see anything of the Taorellis."

It was time to have a showdown talk with Alf. Hewitt
got him aside after supper, sitting on the woodpile with a
glass of whiskey between them.

"Hippo says Hethcutt runs four thousand head of cattle and sometimes five or six hundred horses."

"That's about it."

"How many did he start with?"

"About eight hundred Texas culls."

"Horses?"

"He started out with a good Kentucky stallion and a
string of just average working horses. He knows
horseflesh, and when he started buying brood mares he
got good ones."

"What's on the other side of his place?"

"Rex Patterson's Three Dot."

"What's it like? What's he like?"

"Rex is all right, just shiftless. And he's land-poor. I can
remember when he ran twelve hundred head of cattle
there and needed three times that many more to make the
place pay. I hear he had to mortgage the eight hundred
head he's got now to pay his taxes and the interest on a
loan on his place."

"I see."

"Jeff, what are you getting at?"

"Hethcutt hasn't had access to money enough to pay
cash for what he's got, and he hasn't stolen it all from you
because you never had it. I'd like to know how many Patterson cattle vanished into his herd."

"I've wondered that myself."

"Is there an honest lawyer anywhere near?"

"Tom Pegram, in Three Oaks. Tom's young—well, actually I reckon he's about thirty-three, but he punched cows and read law for a long time and wasn't admitted to the Bar until a couple of years ago."

"Does he represent Hethcutt?"

Whiting snorted. "Hethcutt wouldn't spit on him. His main lawyer is in San Francisco, but there's a fellow in San Luis Obispo—that's the county seat here—who takes care of his local affairs. Man by the name of Fritz Spicer. Used to be a judge back in Ohio or someplace."

"Alf, Hippo and I cornered thirteen Bar H critters while we were on their land today. He roped them one at a time and I looked for your secret check mark. I really had to search, but I found four. Four out of thirteen! Now, a lawyer bold enough to apply that percentage to four thousand—that's a little better than thirty, almost thirty-one, per cent—let's see, you're talking about twelve hundred and forty head."

"Go on."

"Suppose this Rex Patterson filed a suit at the same time—"

Whiting cut in, "Only he didn't check-mark any. That's purely my idee."

"I know, but suppose we file one day, and he files the next, merely applying the same percentage. We're talking about close to twenty-five hundred head of cattle, Alf. What do you think of Tom Pegram as a lawyer?"

"He's smart and he's honest. I like him, and I think he's got guts enough to take it on. How good a lawyer he is—how do I know?"

"What's your opinion of Rex Patterson?"

"We've been friends for years. I could talk him into it. He ain't much, but he's real hard-up, and that can make a difference in a man's backbone."

Whiting took a sip of his whiskey. "But there's one thing you've got to think about, Jeff. Before this gets to the law courts, there will be another kind of trouble, and Hethcutt has got us outgunned."

"I'm sure of that. What would his herd be worth as you ran them out the gate, good and bad together?"

"Oh, up to fifteen dollars apiece."

"Then we're talking about eighteen thousand, six hundred dollars for you, and something like that for Rex Patterson. My company will hire men to fight back. We'll pay the lawyer, and we'll take half of whatever you win above five hundred dollars. How does that deal strike you?"

"Fine. Fair enough."

"Know where you can hire the men?"

"No, but Hippo will."

———————◄◆►———————

Hewitt liked Tom Pegram, who came to Whiting's cabin for a conference and saved them a trip to town. He went through Whiting's notebook a page at a time. Whiting gave him the "Pink Flower" key so it would make sense.

Pegram was a tall, homely man who looked younger than his years. There was a twinkle in his brown eyes except when he looked at Bella Whiting, who ignored him completely. The girl had been going about in Levi's and a shirt, but she put on a dress for the lawyer's appearance, and she set the table and made a pie for their dinner.

To Hewitt it was a little amusing. It was as though she were saying "This is what I could be, but I don't see anything in you to live up to it." She flirted with Hewitt a little. Her father seemed unaware of anything except the notebook and the frown on the young lawyer's face.

Supper over, the table cleared by Bella, they sat around the kitchen table to confer. "The amount of money seems reasonable enough," said Pegram, "if we can get this notebook admitted as evidence and persuade a jury that your stock has been systematically rustled. As I understand it, the dramatic increase in good Shorthorn blood in Hethcutt's herd is the best evidence to back up this log."

"Exactly," said Hewitt. "First time in history a herd of scrubs has been improved without the introduction of good herd bulls."

Pegram frowned. "No use filing for the mere loss. You should demand punitive damages and interest on the lost money. A good round figure, say about fifty thousand dollars."

Whiting's eyes glittered, but he merely nodded.

Pegram went on, "I don't know Rex Patterson and I must not be in the unethical position of soliciting a case. You'll have to talk to him yourself."

"I can take care of that," Whiting said.

"Two other thoughts occur to me. One, you know what's going to happen the minute this suit is filed. They're going to come down on you like a ton of bricks."

Hewitt said, quietly, "I've been in spots like that before. I'll know what to do about it and I'll take the responsibility for it."

"All right, then. The second thing is, there's quite a bit of talk about the Chinese using your place as an opium den. That's irrelevant, and a good judge would throw it out, but it still might influence a jury. People don't give a damn what the Chinese do to each other, but when a white man engages in this trade, with his own daughter in the house, they don't like it."

"I've thought of that, too," Hewitt said, "and I have an idea."

Whiting said, "Lon Tsan has been a friend of mine for

years. I'm not throwing him out for anybody, especially Lionel Hethcutt."

"Then be prepared—" Pegram started to say, but Hewitt held up a hand to interrupt him:

"We can build a little hut in the timber closer to the ocean that will suit Lon Tsan's purpose. Anybody hunting for it would have to pass here, and we ought to maintain a twenty-four-hour guard anyway, once this suit is filed."

"It would be better to eliminate the Chinese factor altogether," Pegram said, "and, officially, I don't want to know what alternative steps you take. You go talk to Patterson and let me know, and meanwhile I'll be preparing the papers for your suit."

"All right," said Whiting. "How are you with a forty-five?"

"I don't know. I've never shot one."

Whiting got up and went to the curtained cabinet in the corner where the dishes were stored. He took out a Colt .45 in a holster and put it on the table in front of the lawyer.

"Before you leave here," he said, "I want you to get used to this gun. Mr. Hewitt may be the best shot in the world with it. He'll be your teacher. You wear that every time you step out on the street in the future. You may not need it, but you'll show them you mean business."

"I'm not sure I like that idea." Pegram pushed back from the table without touching the gun.

Bella Whiting leaned over him to pick up the .45. "If you're afraid of it, I'm not," she said. "I was eleven years old when Dad first started teaching me to use one of these things. Come on outside, and I'll show you."

She dropped the cylinder as she led the way, and spun it to show that there were five cartridges and only one empty chamber. Behind her came her father, then Hewitt, and then a puzzled and reluctant young lawyer. The girl, it seemed to Hewitt, had never looked more feminine and beautiful than she did now, hefting the gun and getting used again to the feel of it.

She looked around to pick out a target. "That yellow rock there," she said, nodding toward one about the size of an orange that lay some twenty feet away.

She thumbed back the hammer, rotating a full chamber into place. She did not close one eye, proof that she had been properly trained. Her whole hand closed carefully on the butt as she squeezed the trigger.

Somehow the report was twice as deafening as if a man had fired it. The big slug struck an inch or two in front of the rock and ricocheted across it. Bella lowered the weapon and handed it to her father, who was carrying the holster.

"I've lost the muscle for it," she said, "but it wouldn't take long to get it back."

Whiting looked at Pegram, who looked at Hewitt a little shamefacedly. "All right, when do you begin coaching me?" he asked.

"Right now, if you've got the time and Alf has the ammunition."

Whiting brought out a full box. "This is one of the reasons I won't cut Lon Tsan off. He gets me all I want of this stuff at half price. I don't know where he gets it and I don't want to know. But one thing I learned in the Army is that nothing is more useless than an empty gun."

Hewitt helped Pegram buckle the holster around him and fill it with twinkling brass cartridges. He had him carry the gun in his hand, to get used to the feel of it, as they walked out into the timber. Not until they were out of sight of the house did they stop.

"That tree yonder will be our target," he said. "Don't

try to hit any given spot on it. Just hit it! Hit a man anywhere with a slug this size and you stop him. Don't jerk
the trigger—do it the way Bella did, and squeeze it with
your whole hand. It's going to try to jump out of your
hand the first time, so be prepared."

The young lawyer lifted the gun, took careful aim, and
fired. Hewitt was not surprised to see him strike the tree,
because his hand and arm had been steady enough. He
had Pegram shoot a dozen rounds and then stopped him
before his hand could become sore from the recoil.

A very sober but slightly more confident lawyer
mounted his horse with a .45 belted to him an hour later.
He tipped his hat to Bella and said good-bye to all of
them, and then rode out of sight. Whiting turned to his
daughter with a smile.

"You had some luck to come that close with your first
shot in—how many years?"

"Five. But it wasn't just luck, Dad. I'm a good shot."

Hewitt said, "A good shot is entitled to a little luck."

She gave him a dazzling smile. "I'd like to see you
shoot."

He shook his head. "When I shoot I mean business."

Hippo returned the next morning with five men. They
were not necessarily men Hewitt would have chosen as
trail companions, but they were tough and steady and
businesslike. Hippo had ridden around the Bar H range to
recruit these men from down in the valley, where they
had been working as farmhands.

"Country down there is going to hell. They're even
raising hogs," one said.

"You won't be working cows for a while," said Hewitt.
"First we're going to have you build a bunkhouse where
you'll be comfortable while you're here. Alf and I have to
be gone for a couple of days. Hippo will be in charge.

There may be a couple of Chinese visitors, but forget you saw them and let Bella take care of them. You just see that nobody prowls the place."

"Right!"

"Another thing—there's a big tomcat puma that has the run of the place. I've found that he won't bother you if you don't bother him. He's not to be bothered, either."

They got the crew started on a bunkhouse the next morning, a log cabin that would have a shingled roof and four windows that would have to be hauled out from Three Oaks. The next day, Hewitt and Whiting hitched up a team, tied two saddled horses on behind the wagon, and headed for the little crossroads town. Hewitt peeled off the money for the shingles and windows, and arranged to leave the team and wagon in the lumberman's yard for a day or two.

They cut across a corner of Hethcutt's range to get to Patterson's Three Dot. The general was well stocked with good cattle. They saw one white-faced Hereford bull, but most of the critters at least could have been descended from Shorthorn sires.

Patterson was a big man, too fat to be as good a man as he once had been, and too discouraged to be impressive, despite having a good mind. He did not catch fire at the idea of suing General Hethcutt but neither did he turn them down.

"Hell, I'll go along with it. Tell the lawyer to fix up the papers and I'll sign 'em," he said. "I figger I can't go on throwing snake eyes the rest of my life."

"You never had any Shorthorn breeding stock, I take it," Hewitt said.

"No, but I've spent eleven years building up a good grade of range beef, selling off my culls and keeping the

best to breed. And somehow I just don't seem to get anywhere. Better critters but not enough of them."

"And you have never suspected someone might be cull-
ing and rustling your best?"

Patterson muttered, "Suspect is one thing. Proving it is
something else."

"How well do you know Hethcutt?"

"For a few years we got along fine. Then he just
stopped neighboring with me after he put up that line
fence."

"I've never seen him. I wonder if the two of you could
describe him well enough for me to draw a pencil portrait
of him. I'm pretty good at it."

They found a large piece of white butcher paper and
held it down on the table while Hewitt sketched at their
directions. "No, a bonier face, not so fleshy. No, more of
an overbearing scowl. Head back more, back stiff as a
poker. That mustache has to be fuller. Not fuzzy—he
takes good care of it—but a lot bigger."

At length they had a picture that satisfied both Whiting
and Patterson. Hewitt studied it a long time.

"Know what strikes me about him?"

"No, what?" said Whiting.

"He looks like the idiot who got his regiment slaugh-
tered at Little Big Horn—George Armstrong Custer."

"Oh, sure," said Patterson. "He's a raving maniac
where Custer is concerned. He thinks Custer got a raw
deal. Best officer the Army ever had—you know!—and
they let the public crucify him after Terry let him down
after ordering him into battle."

"Now we know he's crazier than a bull in fly-time,"
Hewitt said.

"Hell, I could have told you that," said Whiting.

Chapter Four

Hewitt was walking over to where they had built the hut —actually a dugout in the hillside, reinforced with logs and camouflaged with replaced sod—for Lon Tsan and his clients. He was not far from the house when he discovered that Bella Whiting was following him. He stopped and waited for her. She was wearing Levi's, a tight, white shirt, and moccasins, with her hair in braids down her back.

"What's up?" he asked her. She looked like a schoolgirl, but he thought it was pure costumery to soothe her father.

She ran her arm through his. "I just wanted to talk to you, and you never give me a chance. Why do you avoid me all the time?" she asked, plaintively.

It was time to take the bull by the horns. He walked on, letting her cling to his arm but giving her no encouragement.

"Because I'm old enough to be your father," he said.

"Only you're not."

He turned his head and smiled down at her. "And glad of it. I wouldn't want the responsibility of taking care of you right now."

"How about later?"

"Worse still. I'd get older and older and you'd get prettier and prettier. The gap between my judgment and your bullheadedness would get wider and wider."

She thought that over a moment, half smiling. He knew what she was thinking: At least he had admitted that she disturbed him. Suddenly she stopped and made him face her, holding both his arms in her hands.

"Kiss me, Jeff," she said.

He had never been this close to such a winsomely kissable face. He put his arms around her and bent to kiss her briefly and sedately. She melted against him. Her mouth opened for his kiss and her body pressed against his. He had to tear himself away, and still she clung to his arms.

"There you are," he said, keeping as light a tone as he could. "I don't mess around with kids and I don't betray the daughters of my friends."

"But, Jeff," she said, "I'm crazy in love with you and I'm not a kid."

"Bella, I'm not a marrying man. I travel everywhere, places you couldn't go to and wouldn't want to go to. If I went alone and left you here, you'd be miserable, and you'd have a perfect right to be."

"Exactly how old are you?"

"I'll never see forty again."

"The prime of life, and you don't want to travel forever. Dad's getting old, and I'm going to come into some money someday. He'd be the happiest man alive to see you settle down here and—and—you know, take over when it's time for him to rest."

"Take over what? He's got a two-bit spread that will barely support the two of you."

"But if he gets the Bar H, or even a good part of it, it'll be more than he can manage. He'll need help."

"He's figuring on taking over Hethcutt's place?"

"Of course."

Here was something new. Alf Whiting was a deep one,

and a trifle sly. Certainly he had not been entirely frank with Hewitt.

Now was the time to find out a little more, if he could. "How do you get along with your Aunt Bernardina, Mrs. Hethcutt?"

"Oh, fine, only we don't see much of each other. Only when she comes to San Francisco on family visits, when I'm there. Uncle Lionel doesn't admit that I exist."

"How much do you figure on inheriting?"

"Oh, gee, more than a hundred thousand."

"From whom?"

"It's no secret. Aunt Bernardina got her share years ago. I have to wait until I'm twenty-six. It was our share of two Taorelli estates—Grandpa and his brother, Great-uncle Tony. He never married. The Tuscan-American National Bank, in San Francisco, is the trustee. Dad's allowed to draw on the trust for the expenses of raising me, but he has never had to take a cent and it just piles up and piles up."

"What was your grandfather's first name?"

"Frank. What difference does it make?"

"They must have made a wad."

"They were moneylenders during the gold rush, and I don't know what else. What has all this got to do with us?"

"Quite a bit. It's a great relief to me to know that you'll never be in want. When the time comes, I can ride off without a worry in my head."

"Damn!" she said, as he gently disengaged his arms from her grasp. "Jeff, is there someone else?"

"No. I told you, I'm just not a marrying man. I go where my work takes me, and it takes me to some queer places. And that's just the way I like it."

There was a hint of a smile on her pretty face as her

eyes met his. "I wish I knew what you were really up to here. And don't tell me that you're spending all this time on Dad's feud with Uncle Lionel. But I don't care what it is, so long as it keeps you here."

"One thing, Bella. I don't think you have any business going where I'm going now. The less you know of it, the better."

"Oh, hell, I've known about the opium since I was a little girl. Do you think I'm an idiot?"

"Frankly, yes."

She laughed, took his arm again, and began walking along beside him. The hut they had built was only a few hundred yards west of the house. Go a few hundred yards west of it and from a hilltop you could see the ocean. Hippo's crew had shoveled dirt out until they came to a rock deposit that interested Hewitt. He had been around a few quarries, and here were at least a dozen layers of "footing stone," limestone in eight- or ten-inch tiers, a mountain of it.

Easy to quarry, easy to sell. It made good building stone, good riprap for railroad embankments. There was more money here than there was in the cattle business if you knew what to do with it.

So far he had said nothing to Alf Whiting about it. The crew had felled trees and built walls that butted up against the stone face. Over them they had piled the dirt excavated from the hole in the hill. They had mined enough rock to build a front wall and covered it with dirt, too.

It was prominently a scar on the wilderness now, but give it a good winter rain and plant a few more pieces of sod here, and it would vanish into the landscape. You had to know how to find the entrance. He led the way into an almost airtight room about twelve by fourteen, with a log

roof more than eight feet above the dirt floor. Lon Tsan
had already put it to use, and had the bunks for his opium
clients built against the inner wall.

As they came out, the big, male puma, Sneaky, came
gliding down the slope behind them. He was cranky and
suspicious now. It was time for his pipe, and he resented
people denying him what he thought was his.

Nevertheless he came up to the girl and walked along
beside her for a while. She ignored him except when he
pressed against her. Then she scratched his powerful,
tawny back, and he looked up and grumbled as though to
say "What are we waiting for? Why don't you be nice to
me?"

Bella did not let go of Hewitt's arm until they were
near the house again, and by then the lion had left them
to vanish into the brush among the live oak trees. Hippo
and his men were enlarging the bunkhouse and building
more corrals. So far, Hewitt's firm was paying all these
costs, and he winced at the thought of what they would
total by now.

"You think about it," Bella said, in a low voice.

"I shall, but I know what the answer will be."

"One other thing you can think about, Jeff. I want a
new bedroom built on for me, with a bathhouse where I
can heat my own water."

"Suppose we do this. Suppose we build you a bedroom
and build a separate bathhouse, so everyone can use it."

She rolled her eyes at him. "I was thinking of a tub big
enough for two, but not the whole gang."

She gave him that parting thought to occupy him, and
went into the house to prepare the noon meal for the
gang. Her father came riding in just before she was ready
to serve it. Tied behind his saddle was the stout gunny

sack containing his blowtorch and check-mark branding iron.

"Marked six more today," he said. "Two of the heifers have my brand on them, and they're about ready to wean their calves. They're where I can get a rope on them any time you're ready."

"How did you arrange that?" Hewitt asked.

Unsmilingly, Whiting said, "I sowed a couple of hundred acres to oats and put up a few hundred tons of good hay last year. I've been feeding them until they're in the habit of coming back. Jeff, when you're dealing with a sidewinder, you got to be ready to stomp."

◄ ◆ ►

Dressed in his best, Hewitt left the Flying W at daylight the next morning. No one asked any questions and he volunteered no information. Bella was still asleep and Whiting had given the crew breakfast—good bacon, and eggs from his own hens.

Hewitt rode straight east, stopping now and then to make sure he was not being followed. At the wagon road, he paused a long time to make sure it was empty before crossing it. He descended an easy slope to where it became a steep canyon wall. He eased his horse carefully down the wall and then followed the canyon to its mouth.

A hundred yards away ran the tracks of the Southern Pacific. He unbridled his horse and tied her halter rope where she could graze. He lay down and made himself comfortable, dozing off lightly and awakening once when he heard a long freight train puffing up the grade, northbound. He lay down and slept again.

But when a train sounded its whistle far to the north, he awakened instantly and walked out to the edge of the cover of the trees. It was a short passenger train, a local whose last stop had been Paso Robles. He heard the engi-

neer give three quick, soft blasts of the whistle as it began
slowing down, but he did not step out of cover until it
had come to a stop.

The conductor got down and latched the steel plate
that covered the steps. He put his detraining stool down
and offered his hand to the big, florid man who was coming carefully down the steps. The man had to be at least
seventy, and he was carrying too much weight for his
own good.

Behind him came a brakeman carrying two pieces of
luggage. The portly passenger looked around, and Hewitt
showed himself in the edge of the timber. The passenger
said something to the conductor, who tipped his cap as he
threw his stool back into the vestibule and climbed in
after it. One minute later, the train was in motion, gather-
ing speed as it went down the grade.

Hewitt walked out to meet the big man, holding out his
hand. "Mr. Gabrielini?" he said, as they clasped hands.

"Yes, indeed, and you're Mr. Hewitt," the big man said,
without a trace of accent. "This is like the old days, a
sneak meeting in the brush. My first name is Giacomo,
but call me Bill."

"And you already know I'm Jeff."

"Yes, and I'm dying for something to eat. I'm sure you
didn't come prepared, but I did. If you can assist me by
carrying that square case—"

Hewitt picked up the case, which was the size of a
small steamer trunk, with a suitcase handle as well as
trunk handles on the end. "I'm sorry, but we're quite a
way from water," he said, as he led the way back into the
shelter of the trees.

"Who drinks water?"

They went far enough back to be invisible from the
track. Hewitt put the case down. Mr. Giacomo Gabrielini,

president of the Tuscan-American National Bank of San Francisco, huffed and puffed as he knelt to take charge. He stood well over six feet tall, but he surely weighed close to three hundred pounds. He was dressed in a business suit and derby, and he wore congress gaiters. His hair was white, his complexion fair, and his eyes a deep blue. He was clean-shaven.

He opened the trunk and displayed a handsome picnic lunch—crusty bread, several kinds of sausage and cheese, some grapes and a cantaloupe, and two big bottles of wine. There were big, white napkins, real silver, and fine big goblets for the wine.

And it was an excellent red wine, Hewitt decided after a single sip. He took the knife Gabrielini offered and cut himself a chunk of sausage, one of cheese, and one of bread. The banker poured the wine and held his glass up in a toast.

"Success," he said.

"I can drink to that."

They drank. Gabrielini seemed to be in no hurry to get down to business. He ate as though he enjoyed every morsel. He would, Hewitt thought, quickly eat himself into his grave.

"It's a very touchy affair," he said. "I could think of no other way to arrange a meeting with you."

"Lon Tsan brought me your note last week," said Hewitt.

"Good man, Lon Tsan. Before I forget it, here is a letter from your office."

There was no mistaking Conrad Meuse's strong penmanship, deep, black ink and logical, methodical brevity of style—even though this was probably the longest letter Hewitt had ever received from him. But what struck Hewitt first was the new letterhead:

Bankers Bonding and Indemnity Company
Conrad Meuse   *Jefferson Hewitt*
Corner Suite 2 & 3
Above
STOCKMEN'S NATIONAL BANK OF CHEYENNE

Well! Same old, familiar office quarters, but Stockmen's
was now a national bank, not a state bank, and it had
moved lock, stock, and barrel into the lower floor of the
building occupied by BB&I. Hewitt excused himself to
read Conrad's letter:

My dear Jefferson:
First, you will observe the new address. We have
cashed out the mining interests in South Dakota and
the timber interests in California, both investments
on which I heartily congratulate you. We have
bought a 40% interest in the Stockmen's Bank and
both of us are on the board of directors. Thanks to
the infusion of new money from our above profits, we
were able to increase the capitalization of the bank
by $150,000. I hope you approve.

And a hell of a lot of good it would do me to disapprove
from here, Hewitt thought. . . . He read on.

The case on which you are now engaged is more
complex, and probably much bigger, than either of
us anticipated. We are of course bondsmen for Tuscan-American National Bank of San Francisco,
whose president, Giacomo Gabrielini, will explain
our interest. Mr. Gabrielini has been my guest here
in Cheyenne several times and I have the highest respect for his integrity and acumen, as well as a deep
friendship for him.

My inquiries about brevet Brigadier General Hethcutt, U.S.A. Retd., produced some curious contradictions. I may say he always had the reputation for shady dealing as a junior officer. I speculate when I say that he created the opportunity for illegal peculation by his superiors when he had reason to fear a court-martial. For no other reason was he permitted to resign with his record intact.

It is clear that Sergeant Whiting was deeply involved in the same affair, but the records have been purged where he is concerned, and he was given a medical discharge due to a heart condition. Whole sheafs of pages on this investigation have simply disappeared. One source told me that it was a classical case of "passing the buck" upward, to protect high-ranking officers and thus save himself. I hesitate to commit details to a letter, but you can rely on Mr. Gabrielini to give you the facts. His bank is endangered to the extent of some $250,000, and I rely on you to proceed with your usual delicacy and tact. I personally will negotiate the fee for our services after you have cleared up the case. With warmest regards, I am,

Your obdt. servant,
Conrad Meuse.

Gabrielini was holding out a box of cigars to Hewitt and saying, "Indian, not Cuban. Different but I trust you will enjoy them. I also brought along a flask of Bourbon, since I understand that Bourbon is your drink."

Hewitt downed a good shot of excellent whiskey and puffed away at an excellent cigar as he reread Conrad's letter. He folded the letter and put it in his pocket as

Gabrielini indicated that he was to help himself, meanwhile pouring two glasses of red wine.

Hewitt cut off a piece of bread and a piece of sausage and put them on a napkin on his lap. "Well, sir?" he said.

The Italian banker chuckled. "An excellent opening, my dear Hewitt. I'll condense as much as possible. As the Indian wars wound down, a great deal of surplus equipment was collected in Phoenix, Sacramento, and Stockton to be sold. My bank got into it when General Hethcutt wanted to borrow seventy-five thousand with which to buy much of this stuff."

"What stuff?"

"Oh—horses and mules, mostly. But also wagons, mess gear from big pots to portable stoves to mess kits. Guns and ammunition. Blankets. Tents, large and small. Even flagpoles and guy wires."

"What did Hethcutt propose to do with it?"

"Retail most of it at a considerable profit, but keep enough to equip a cattle operation he was then negotiating to buy."

"The Bar H?"

"Yes, only it was then the Eighty-Eight."

"He was married at the time?"

"He married Bernardina Taorelli shortly before he retired."

"And I imagine this is where Whiting came in."

"More or less. The fraud actually had been going on for years. A purchase order would show that one horse had been bought at the top price, and the inventory would show one horse. However *two* horses—or mules, as the case may be—were actually delivered, and one never went on inventory. Likewise with wagons, tents, and other field equipment."

"And Sergeant Whiting was in charge of the Records Section, I would imagine."

"Correct. The Army was feeding some one hundred and ten horses and thirty-odd mules not on inventory, and storing some fifty thousand dollars' worth of equipment that also was not on inventory. When many of the horses and mules were declared surplus, Whiting had more than two hundred and fifty to dispose of. Approximately the same ratio of equipment. Altogether nearly two hundred thousand dollars' worth of government property, if you include that which had never been carried on the records."

"Too much for an enlisted man to handle," Hewitt murmured.

"Exactly. He had been too successful too long. It was a staff man, Major Fred Herbert, who felt he had enough evidence to file charges. General Hethcutt had just been transferred from Arizona Territory to San Francisco for processing of his retirement. In short, Whiting knew enough about his scandalous reputation to go straight to him and offer to split the deal if he could handle Major Herbert. I imagine there was some dickering, because Whiting was confined to quarters for a week—although that now doesn't appear on the records, either.

"Whiting had his convenient heart attack and was discharged. He alone knew where the loot was, and Hethcutt had to trust him to dispose of it. I don't know who else was in on it, but Hethcutt came out of it with a little more than seventy thousand dollars and Whiting fifteen thousand and thirty-four head of unbranded horses."

"About the right split, considering rank," Hewitt murmured.

Gabrielini ate greedily but drank daintily. "I imagine so. Whiting apparently had been cashing in a little here and there over the years, because he bought the Flying W property for cash—twenty-one thousand dollars—and he paid cash for some purebred bulls and some good breeding cows. There went another ten or fifteen thousand."

"And the Army just sat there and let it happen?"

"My dear Mr. Hewitt, the conspiracy had long reached far up into the War Department itself. Some influential citizens later kicked themselves when they found out how much had been available, and they had settled for so little. But what could they do?"

"How did Hethcutt and Whiting fall out?"

"They never really did. They detested each other but needed each other, and there had been no personal attachment on either side. But the general married Bernardina Taorelli. At thirty-eight she was the eldest of five Taorelli girls. Wealthy family, quite modern and Americanized, hands into everything that makes money. At one time, the general came to me to discuss buying a wholesale grocery house in San Francisco, but I couldn't encourage it because it was in bad shape."

"How did a mere sergeant marry into the Taorelli family?"

"You may be assured it was not sanctioned by the family in the conventional sense. Zoe was the youngest, only twenty-four. She and Whiting went for a steamer trip up to Sacramento and then for a week's vacation in the Sierra Nevada somewhere. Everyone knew about it—Zoe saw to that. When they came back, the Taorellis were happy to settle for a marriage, especially when Whiting bought this property so close to San Francisco.

"And then General Hethcutt heard that the old Eighty-Eight ranch was for sale. I think he bought it, hoping to gobble up Whiting, get rid of him once and for all. Whiting will always be a potential witness against Hethcutt, the one man who can blast his reputation. In fact he's in a position to claim he was merely taking orders, that a mere sergeant could not defy a brigadier general. He'd come out of it a martyr."

"Where does your bank come in?"

"Through the suckers' gate. We loaned Hethcutt fifty thousand when he bought the ranch. We loaned him another fifty thousand to improve it—fences, buildings, breeding cattle, more horses—you know! I had a man investigate and I doubt that twenty thousand actually went into the ranch, and most of that went on the big house he built."

The banker fell silent. Hewitt merely waited, knowing how painful it must be. In a moment, Gabrielini went on, slowly, "Then the Taorellis formed a combine to buy and consolidate a number of businesses in San Francisco. Naturally, Hethcutt was a member of the syndicate. I should have known better when Ferguson, Hall and Schmidt, Incorporated, turned up as one of the firms to be bought. That was the wholesale grocers Hethcutt had wanted to buy. It was bankrupt, but the Taorellis had such big plans for it! When old Antonio Taorelli, brother of Frank, who was Zoe and Bernardina's grandfather, died, we had been made trustees for the estate. He left a net estate of nearly three quarters of a million.

"It is hard to assume the worst in circumstances like those. To make a long story short but no less heartbreaking, the bank was in for another hundred and fifty thousand before the syndicate finally went bankrupt. Not one cent was salvaged—not one!"

"I see. You're a quarter of a million down, then."

"You do not see. It is worse than that. We invested the funds of the Tony Taorelli trust in that damned syndicate because it looked so rich and promised to make the girls some money. The terms of the trust indenture called for investment only in A-rated public bonds. We have to pay out the income of the trust to the beneficiaries and we have already paid out some thirty thousand in nonexistent profits. Somehow we have to replace that, plus nearly six hundred thousand of the vanished corpus.

"Mr. Hewitt, we are half a million short, and our reputation in two worlds—the financial and the Italian—totters on the brink. That is why you are here."

Hewitt felt a distinct chill. He doubted that the bank's officials had been bonded by his and Conrad's company for any such amount, but surely at least a quarter of a million of their own money was at stake. Whatever the amount, Conrad had written the bond on the basis of financial reports and analyses—and, indeed, Gabrielini and his bank did have a spotless reputation. They were known all over the West.

"Mr. Gabrielini," he said, "who has the money now?"

"I wish I knew."

"Just tell me whom you suspect. It wasn't burned up in a fire. It didn't just vanish like mist in a breeze. Somebody is sitting on a pile of loot. Give me a name!"

Gabrielini took out a big handkerchief and, with trembling hands, mopped a forehead and face that had suddenly gone slick with sweat. He had to force his eyes to meet Hewitt's.

"Not the Taorellis. They are an honest family. There was one, just one, profitable company in the syndicate—Li Fang Importing Company. From an informant there—"

"His name wouldn't be Lon Tsan, would it?"

The banker nodded. "He is the most honest, the most reliable businessman I know. Odd, isn't it, that an illegal business like opium should be used as a cover-up to pursue the honest purpose of recovering this loot? It was Lon

Tsan's own idea. His family's name, too, is tarnished by this bankruptcy, and he won't rest until he has cleared it."

"Whom does he think has the money?" When Gabrielini remained silent, Hewitt pressed him. "It's Hethcutt, isn't it? He probably had to pay off a few people here and there, but he's sitting on most of the loot, just as he is the army loot—right?"

The banker looked off into the distance. "I have utilized every resource at my command to try to determine that, and failed. Yet the conviction remains that he is one of the worst scoundrels in the world. It's more than just a feeling. Have you met the man?"

"I have not had that privilege."

"He's an egotistical madman. Once shortly after his wedding we went to lunch at my club, and he had a little too much to drink. He said that within five years he meant to be a millionaire. Yes, sir, he looked me right in the eye and boasted that he was going to rob me of enough to give him a million. It gives me cold shivers to remember it."

Gabrielini's eyes blazed. Hewitt waited for the man to collect his thoughts. "And by God," Gabrielini went on, when he had done so, "he almost made his drunken boast good. *He almost did it!* At the War Department's expense. At his own in-laws' expense. At the expense of Chinese businessmen who trusted him because he had married into the Taorellis. And at *my* expense! That's what humiliates me."

"What's his wife like?"

"I hardly know. She used to be a plain, sweet, not very pretty woman. You know—born to be a nun. For a while, being married to a brigadier general seemed to go to her head. She was the first of the old families to marry a non-Italian, you know. I haven't seen her in three or four years."

"But what have you heard?"

"That she has become reclusive, a shrew, a woman who hides from the world in a big ranch house where only a personal maid sees her."

"She goes to San Francisco to see her family, doesn't she? Bella said she met her there."

"Two years ago, when her brother died, was the last time. Mr. Hewitt, all my resources having failed, I have to ask you how you plan on attacking this case?"

"There's only one thing to do. When you can't find the handle, you push. You push here and you push there, until something gives. Alf Whiting and another fellow and I are preparing a lawsuit that will perhaps blast Hethcutt out into the open. Whiting is nobody's fool, believe me."

"Oh, I believe you! But watch your backs, both of you. Lon Tsan says that Hethcutt has hired a gang of professional murderers that—"

"I know all about that. I know how to deal with them. What else about Hethcutt—how would he hide the loot? What form would it be in? What, in short, am I looking for? Cash? Stocks and bonds? What?"

"He collected precious stones, I know, and owned thirty or forty thousand dollars' worth of diamonds when he and Bernardina were married. He had a tiara made for her for a wedding present. He really doesn't know much about stocks, bonds, and securities. There are great gaps in his knowledge."

A northbound train was whistling distantly, puffing up the grade toward them. The banker took out the big watch in his vest pocket and exclaimed, "My God, look what time it is! I'm afraid I'm going to have to leave my hamper with you and just take my suitcase and run for it."

They barely made it to the rails in time to flag the train to San Francisco. Gabrielini looked much relieved as he waved farewell to Hewitt from the steps of the passenger car, but Hewitt could not share his optimisim.

Neither could he appear at Alf Whiting's ranch with the fine hamper and the fine food it contained. Had Whiting suspected that he had been in conference with the banker, no telling what his reaction would be. Hewitt scattered the bread and cheese so the wild creatures of the forest could eat it. He hid the hamper in a tree whose foliage would conceal it, and waited until he was closer to the house before burying the unopened bottle of wine.

The last of the sausage—a pound and a half—he saved until he saw Sneaky lonesomely prowling the corrals. He needed to firm up his relations with the lion anyway. He cut the sausage into chunks and tossed them to the puma and then let the cat lick the hands that had held it. Sneaky walked all the way to the kitchen door with him, pressing against his leg and making that sound, something like a gas engine with a broken exhaust valve running down, that passed for a purr with him. Bella had to slap him in the face with the side of the broom to keep him out of the house.

Chapter Five

Hewitt had seen San Luis Obispo only once, and had fallen in love with it. It was built on a slope around an old Franciscan mission, almost within sight of the sea. But all these California towns were changing so rapidly that he hardly recognized the place.

There was no sign of the Bar H crew at the courthouse. "Didn't expect it," Alf Whiting said. "You can count on His Nibs waiting to parade the troops when it will make the biggest impression. Hewitt, my daughter will stay with our friends the Andersons for today. You take her there."

Bella had come to town in a blue riding skirt, with a little beret cocked on her mass of black curls. She was riding the best horse her father owned, and riding it well. Her color was high, her eyes sparkling. She had never looked so attractive.

She peeled off the procession, letting Hewitt catch up and ride beside her. "The Andersons used to own part of Dad's ranch," she said. "They're like grandparents to me."

"Well, they won't be ashamed of the way you look today," Hewitt replied.

"I'll tell them we're engaged." Hewitt only grunted; so she went on, "I'll tell them Daddy caught us in bed together, and it's a have-to case."

"Bella," he said, "there's a time for teasing and a time to be serious. This is a damned serious lawsuit."

"Oh, I'm serious too!"

He lost his temper a little, the first sign of the inner tension that was building up in him. "One of these days," he said, "I'm going to paddle you good and hard, the way you deserve."

"Oh, that'll be fun!"

It was a losing proposition. He remained silent the rest of the way to the Andersons' house. He dismounted and was introduced to the old couple, but he did not go in, and, much to his relief, Bella was demurely proper.

He returned to the courthouse. Still no sign of Hethcutt's forces, but Tom Pegram was in the corridor with Whiting and the Flying W men. He signaled to a short, plump man in a business suit, but wearing a wide-brimmed hat and cowboy boots.

"Opposing counsel," he murmured to Hewitt. He laid his hand on the plump man's arm and said, "Mr. Spicer, allow me to present Mr. Jefferson Hewitt. Jeff, Counselor Fritz Spicer, who represents General Hethcutt."

Spicer was sharp-eyed, suspicious. "Understand you work for Bankers Bonding and Indemnity Company, of Cheyenne," he said as he shook hands.

Hewitt wondered where he could have heard that news. "No, I don't work for them. I'm one of the partners," he said.

Spicer raised his eyebrows. "Rather small potatoes, this case, for a man in your position."

"Oh, small potatoes grow to be big ones."

"Private detectives aren't well thought of around here."

"Meaning?"

"It puzzles me that a partner would risk his own and his firm's reputation in something like this."

The man was trying the old poker player's trick of gouging for a tender nerve before a single card had been dealt. It was time to gouge back.

"Frankly, Judge," he said, "I've been puzzled why a man in your position would risk your reputation as a legal scholar, appearing for a pip-squeak who is hiring professional gunmen to do his dirty work for him."

"I resent that, sir! What professional gunman do you mean?"

"I'll give you one name for a starter. Oscar Hyde, otherwise known as 'Crazy Ozzie.' Have you met him?"

"No, sir, but—"

"I thought not. When you do, try to picture yourself up there in open court, trying to defend him with your family looking on. I think you'll see what I mean."

"I believe I've had enough of this, Mr. Hewitt," Spicer said, stiffly. "Nice to have met you."

"The pleasure is mutual."

As Spicer turned away, Hewitt saw a slender man in a gray business suit cross the corridor, going from one county office to another. He wore a wide-brimmed hat that shaded his face, but there was no question about it—the man was Lon Tsan. Hewitt hid a smile. Mr. Giacomo Gabrielini meant to have his own sources of information on this hearing.

They could hear horsemen coming down the street. Hewitt cautioned the others to remain where they were, but he went to the front doors at the end of the corridor to look out. There were eleven riders, and the man in front was small enough to play Napoleon. But he wore the flowing hair and mustache—and somehow the very expression—of George Armstrong Custer, who would go down in history as the blunderer who got the entire 7th

Cavalry exterminated by Indians at the Battle of the Little Big Horn.

He wore a blue-checked, long-sleeved shirt with a dark blue kerchief caught up in a silver clip. He had on military gauntlets, black pants, and high-heeled boots with small, shining spurs. He sat his saddle erectly, ignoring the rank and file that rode behind him.

Hewitt had no trouble picking out Crazy Ozzie Hyde. These riffraff troublemakers who tried to create their own legends were a familiar type. They never worked long enough or hard enough to accumulate decent clothing and always looked dirty and unkempt. This specimen was a small man, gaunt to emaciation, with almost no chin and a small, tight, angry mouth.

There were two or three others on the Bar H crew that could have passed themselves off as gunmen, had not Crazy Ozzie already pre-empted the title. There were far fewer such scofflaws than there had been even ten years ago, but they still existed, and Hewitt had only contempt for them. That they struck terror in the hearts of better men only infuriated him.

He returned to Alf Whiting, Tom Pegram, and the others. Pegram was looking a little nervous. "I wonder," he said, "if we shouldn't be sitting in the courtroom, waiting, when they come in?"

Hewitt looked at his watch. It was still thirty minutes before court time. "Why?" he said.

"Well, we don't want to leave our case out here in the hall, and that's what could happen if they try to bully us."

"They won't bully me," said Hippo Thompson.

"Nor me," said Alf Whiting. "You watch—old Hethcutt is going to have to empty his bladder first thing. Hell of a way to start a court case."

He seemed completely serene as the Bar H crew filed

in behind their leader. And sure enough, they heard General Hethcutt ask loudly, "Where's the gents' room? Have to see a man about a dog."

Somebody pointed. Hethcutt went through the door, removing his gauntlets. His men circled in front of it, as though standing guard on his privacy. It occurred to Hewitt that here might be a good chance to gouge at a tender nerve.

"How about it, Crazy Ozzie, don't you have to go in and button him up again?" he called.

The little man spun on his heel, his eyes glittering. "Who said that?" he snarled.

"I did," said Hewitt. "I thought you were the official back scratcher on the Bar H."

Before the vicious little gunman could say anything, Judge Spicer came hurrying past the Whiting partisans with his hand up, palm out. "Don't let yourselves be baited into trouble, men," he said. "This is Jeff Hewitt, a private detective and a trick circus shot. Just ignore him."

"I'll ignore him, all right," said Hyde.

Spicer shook his finger at him. "I mean it. You men let yourselves be talked into a fight in the corridor, and I'll tell the general he can get someone else to represent him."

Hethcutt came out of the men's room then. "What's this all about?" he demanded.

Spicer, without looking back, pointed at Hewitt. "That man in the ruffled white shirt is Jefferson Hewitt, of Bankers Bonding and Indemnity Company. He's notorious as a gunman and what he's going to try to do is bait somebody into drawing on him. General, I was just warning your men that if they fall for it, I will withdraw from the case."

"Gutless," Hethcutt said, without emotion. But he

turned to his men and said, "This is an order. Go into the courtroom and sit down, and ignore that Pinkerton. Let's go."

But as he passed the Flying W crew, it was not Whiting he examined, but Hewitt. He looked at him contemptuously, the downward glance of a martinet who never for a fraction of a second was unaware of his rank. Hewitt had known very good officers, very bad officers, and many an officer in between. This was one of the bad ones.

But it was still time to gouge. He waited until they had passed and then said, loudly, "I wonder if he makes his wife salute before she gets into bed?"

Hethcutt had started to turn into the courtroom. He whirled on his heel, his face going white. Probably, Hewitt thought, he was wondering what Hewitt knew of his relations with his wife, and who else knew it.

Whatever he had been about to say, he thought better of it. He went into the courtroom, and for a moment the entire building was quiet. Then Pegram signaled for them to follow him.

The Bar H crew had sat down on the right-hand side of the aisle. Pegram motioned for the Flying W to take the side to the left. Hewitt let the others edge in first, so he could sit on an aisle seat directly across from Crazy Ozzie Hyde.

In front of the room, on the other side of the railing, Pegram and Whiting were sitting down at a table to the left; Spicer and Hethcutt already sat at one at the right. A middle-aged deputy sheriff, the court's bailiff, stood at attention immediately in front of the bench, his arms crossed behind his back.

Hewitt leaned across the aisle. "Where have you been spending the last year or so, Ozzie? I haven't heard much of you," he said, genially.

"You don't know me and I don't know you," Hyde said.

"Oh yes, you may not know me, but I make it my business to keep track of chicken thieves like you. I've got quite a file on your type. Yours isn't very thick, though, because you've never done much but bluff."

"You son of a bitch—"

The deputy sheriff took a step forward. He could not have heard the words but he could not help but know that something disquieting to the peace of the court was going on. He held up a hand to get their attention.

"Gentlemen, all of you!" he said, loudly. "I'm going to require that you all give me your guns before court opens. You'll get them back as soon as court adjourns. We'll start with the two principals in the case."

Whiting shot to his feet and unbuckled his gun belt. "Sure, Ollie, and excuse me for not thinking of it," he said. "Just habit, I reckon."

Hethcutt got up and took a Colt .45 from his holster and handed it over, butt forward. There was nothing the two crews could do then but hand over their guns, too. The deputy had them stacked on his arm like firewood when he went into the judge's chambers behind the bench.

He returned, and in a moment called out, "Hear ye, hear ye, this honorable superior court of San Luis Obispo County in the state of California is now open. Will you please rise. The Honorable James Towers presiding. Please sit down."

Judge Towers did not wear robes. He was not a large man, nor was there anything impressive physically about him. He was obviously an easterner, however, and the fact that he still dressed the way he had "back home" indicated to Hewitt how he felt about things. He would run

this court the way he thought it should be run, and anyone who didn't like it could appeal to a higher court.

There were no spectators other than the two crews.
Hethcutt's lawyer had unexpectedly proposed that they
waive a jury and let the judge decide. Tom Pegram had
accepted with as much alacrity as surprise. Hewitt
thought he knew why the offer had been made. Rank!
The general did not want ordinary men deciding his des-
tiny and he could not conceive of a country judge ruling
against him.

Not even the sheriff was present, but Whiting had pre-
dicted this. Sheriff Macklin Hale was a gutless politician
who conveniently became ill whenever a real crisis might
force him to take sides. He was ill today.

The stately preliminaries that seemed to take up so
much of a court's time did not last long with Judge
Towers. Almost before Hewitt realized it, it was time for
Tom Pegram to start putting on his case.

Pegram arose. Good, thought Hewitt, he's got a good
courtroom voice . . . !

"We have charged damages by reason of criminal
theft," Pegram said, "and I now propose to make an offer
of proof in the form of a stipulation. Mr. Hethcutt—excuse
me, *General* Hethcutt—has some six hundred steers, up to
three years old, confined in a fence pasture near his
house.

"If we can adjourn this court to that pasture, my client
has a way of proving that theft has occurred, and a mathematical formula by which the court can determine the
size of the theft over the years. We will furnish the man-
power to make the examination, and we will leave it to
the court to decide on the validity of whatever evidence it
educes.

"If we are successful, as I am sure we will be, I will

make the same offer of proof in Patterson *versus* Hethcutt when it comes on for trial. I now hand a copy of my proposed stipulation to the court and to opposing counsel, and if defense agrees, I move that it be made an order of this court."

He handed documents to the judge and to Spicer. The judge frowned as he read his, and then read it again. Spicer and Hethcutt put their heads together to read theirs. Spicer rose to his feet.

"There's been a lot of talk about Shorthorn blood in this case, your honor," he said. "If that is the test plaintiff proposes, I should like to ask how he plans to prove what breed of cattle these are."

"The Shorthorn blood is a side issue that may or may not be relevant, sir," Pegram said, addressing the court. "I would not, at this point, bring up the issue. I may, however, do so at a later date."

"What I want to know," said the judge, "is what kind of magical test you've got in mind. Are these all branded cattle?"

"I believe so, sir. They all bear Mr. Hethcutt's—excuse me, *General* Hethcutt's—Bar H brand."

"A brand sufficiently identifies the property in this state, Mr. Pegram."

"Not if it has been illegally and feloniously applied to someone else's critter, if it please the court."

Hethcutt shot to his feet. "Illegally?" he choked. "Feloniously? Do you realize that you're accusing me of cattle rustling?"

"Yes, sir, I do, and I propose to prove it if you have the nerve to sign this stipulation."

"You can't go behind a brand. That's the purpose of the damned thing. Any cow branded with my brand is my cow. Any steer branded with my brand is my steer—"

Spicer was tugging at his coattails to make him sit down. The judge was rapping lightly with his gavel. Hethcutt realized where he was, and fell silent. The judge pointed the gavel at him.

"Am I to understand that you reject this offer of proof, then?"

"Of course, unless we know what kind of proof he's talking about."

The judge looked at Pegram, who said, "Proof that this court will accept. Proof that any court will accept. The fact that the method has never been used before does not invalidate it. We propose to offer the cattle business an entirely new way of validating a brand, and a court should supervise its first test and rule on its acceptability—"

On and on and on, quietly goading General Hethcutt with the unspoken inference that he was afraid to submit to any test of any kind. He even said, "In all my experience with army officers I have never known one who feared the unknown. Retreat in the face of overwhelming odds is one thing, but to fall back precipitately simply because he does not know what is in front of him is not characteristic of our Army."

Yes sir, this boy would go far in the legal profession. He was getting to Hethcutt. What was more important, he was getting to the judge. He said a lot in a few words and sat down. The judge looked over at Spicer.

"I confess that I am curious about anything that can protect a cattleman's rights against rustlers," he said, "but I fail to see how this court can order you to accept the test or abide by its findings."

Hethcutt was whispering so loudly that he was spraying Spicer's ear with spittle. The attorney stood up.

"Well, your honor," he said, "let us have this little test.

Quite frankly, sir, I like to see a young fellow display bold ingenuity in court, and I compliment counsel on it."

The rest was easy and quick. Tomorrow court would convene in the Bar H pasture at ten o'clock in the morning. Hethcutt was furious, but it had been Hewitt's experience that no general ever expected to be proved wrong, and by the glitter in his eye the general was looking forward to the humiliation of the enlisted man who had had the gall to marry into his wife's family.

They waited until Spicer and Hethcutt and their men had been given back their guns. The deputy then brought out the ones remaining, to be claimed by Whiting's men. The judge leaned on his elbow on the bench, watching with a smile.

Pegram bowed to him before turning toward the courtroom door. Hewitt did likewise.

"One moment, Mr. Hewitt," the judge said.

"Sir?" Hewitt said, stopping to face him.

"Didn't you appear as a witness in a case, I forget the name but I believe it was something like Houseman, in New Mexico Territorial Court some years back?"

"Why, yes, your honor, yes I did," Hewitt said. "I think your honor refers to the murder charge against Carl Hauser, who was found not guilty."

"Largely on your testimony."

"I had reason at the time to hope so."

The judge crooked his finger to Hewitt to come forward to the bench. He leaned across to speak in a low voice.

"I'm a little baffled by this offer of proof," he said. "I would feel better if I had your assurance that you personally believe in it."

"I do, your honor. I believe it will require some amount of inductive reasoning on the court's part, but while I'm not a student of the law, I feel it will add something to the science of jurisprudence."

The judge merely nodded, a nod that said both "Thank you" and "Good-bye" as well as "Don't try to take advantage of this." They passed out into the sunshine, where the Bar H crew was preparing to mount up.

Hewitt kept his eye on the man called, behind his back at least, Crazy Ozzie. Ozzie was in the saddle when his unreliable temper gave way. He slid out of the saddle with the swiftness of a snake and came running toward Hewitt.

"Say whatever you've got to say to me out here in public," he shouted. "Damn your soul to hell, say it and I'll cram it down your throat."

Hewitt had already lost the advantage of distance. He knew he was a better shot than nine out of ten men, and he would not have feared Crazy Ozzie in the slightest at the maximum range of a .45. Now his only chance was to get the man still closer.

"How about I whisper it in your dirty little ear?" he said.

Hyde jumped for him, yanking out his gun. Hewitt jumped too, hearing the gun blast in his ear as the slug went screeching past his head. He hooked his heel behind the heel of Ozzie's boot and kicked backward.

Ozzie went down. Hewitt got his hand on Ozzie's gun arm and twisted it, seeing men scatter in all directions as the muzzle of the weapon wavered a full circle. Hewitt reached into his hip pocket and brought out the limber little leather-covered, shot-filled sap that was his favorite weapon.

He did not swing it. He snapped it, using the power of his wrist instead of his arm. He caught Ozzie on the biceps of his right arm, paralyzing the whole arm. The gun dropped to the sidewalk.

Hewitt stood up, jerked Ozzie to his feet, and tapped him lightly on the side of his head with the sap. The evil little gunman went limp. Gently, Hewitt lowered him to the sidewalk and then kicked the man's .45 far out into the street.

"General," he said to Hethcutt, "I think your sign just fell over."

As they rode out of town, Whiting and his daughter in the lead, Hewitt caught Hippo Thompson studying him with an air of embittered concentration. "That the fellow who mauled you around, Hippo?" he asked.

The big man sighed and seemed to awaken from a dream. "Yes," he said, "and then he held a gun on me while a couple of others worked me over. You know, don't you, that he can't let this drop?"

Hewitt shrugged. "Why do you think I did it that way? He'll have his mind on his job now, not the general's. They're a pair of peaches, aren't they?"

Hippo saw nothing funny in it. "I'll cover your back, Mr. Hewitt," he said, "but when the flag goes up, I want that little bastard all to myself."

"You want to be the man who killed Crazy Ozzie Hyde, is that it?"

"No, I learned something today, watching you. What I want to be is the man that rubbed his nose in the dirt and made him like it."

Hewitt grinned. "You're catching on."

Chapter Six

Tom Pegram had done his homework. He was far more at home in the saddle than his opponent, Judge Spicer, and he not only knew the cattle business better, he had accumulated a mass of figures showing how the Hethcutt herds had grown over the past few years. Hewitt liked his approach to the case. He seemed to expect to win it, and self-confidence was half the battle.

"Before we begin our demonstration," he said, "I should like to ask General Hethcutt a question or two."

"Subject to the court's ruling on relevancy," Judge Towers said quickly, before Spicer could intervene.

"Certainly." Pegram waved his hand to indicate the fenced pasture, which Hewitt estimated to contain no more than three hundred acres. "I wish to ask first if there is anything special about the cattle held here. That is, are they culls? Are they selected breeding stock? Are they to be shipped or sold, anything like that?"

No one had dismounted. Spicer spun his horse so that he could lean over and confer in whispers with his client. After a moment he turned his horse to face the judge.

"I have no objection to answering those questions, although it sounds odd to me to hear steers referred to as 'breeding stock,'" he said.

"Well, I happened to notice a few females," said Pegram, "so I'll leave the question as I framed it. Will the witness answer?"

General Hethcutt said—barked, rather—"There's nothing to distinguish these cattle from others I own. I had too many on the north range. When I began to move some of them down to fresh grass, I tried to pick steers that will go to market later this summer or fall. The reason is that they will be nearer to the railroad and reduce my roundup costs. We picked up a few cows, I suppose, but whether I ship them or keep them will depend on how they look at the time."

"Very good, sir," said Pegram. "Then these are neither better nor worse than the average run of the quality of your herds."

"About the same."

"How many head do you own, altogether?"

"I object," Spicer said. "The offer of proof concerned the ones held here."

"I will withdraw the question," said Pegram, "although when I am able to establish relevancy I will probably ask it again. One more question of this witness. The Bar H brand on these critters was applied by your crews, at your direction?"

"Yes. I give the orders here." General Hethcutt was still barking in his command voice.

"Very good. I now wish to introduce an exhibit which consists of two parts. Mr. Whiting, if you please."

Whiting dismounted and took the old gunny sack from behind his saddle and opened it. He took out the short check-mark brand with the wooden T handle and the alcohol blowtorch.

"I will ask Mr. Whiting to tell me the purpose of these tools and then ask that they be admitted as exhibits," Pegram said.

"I was pretty broke after losing my wife," Whiting said. "Her last illness cleaned me out of cash. When I went to find cattle I could sell, and I had to do it almost by myself because I couldn't afford to hire riders, I found out that I had fewer than I had three and four years earlier. I hadn't sold a damn critter except a couple of young crossbred breeding bulls, but I was nearly eight hundred head short."

"You had no intimation that your herd had been decreasing?"

"Like I said, my wife was dying and I didn't take much interest in anything else. I took note that I had better grass than I had any right to expect, but it wasn't until after she died that I used my last money to hire a few hands and run a count. That's when I found that some damned thief had been rustling my calf crop for several years. All I had left was old cows and my bulls."

"These were good cows?"

"The best I had. I'd culled down pretty hard and sold off the culls to pay my medical bills."

"You never had any Galloway or Aberdeen-Angus stock?"

"I never had a black critter on the place."

"Did General Hethcutt?"

"He used to have quite a few of them. He came here to start breeding Galloways."

"Of your own knowledge, how many black or partly black cattle does he own now?"

"I'd have to estimate it at forty or fifty, and they're only partly black. A Galloway bull is pretty expensive now, and they're a polled breed."

"You mean they have no horns."

"Yes."

"Aren't there polled Shorthorns, too?"

"Yes, but they're a separate breed. I went for the horned breed because you can breed them up to where their horns are longer, and I bought horned cow stock, too."

"For what purpose?"

"We've still got wolves and pumas and bears around here, and a polled critter can't defend itself. I wanted bulls that could defend their herds."

"Did you ever discuss this with General Hethcutt?"

"I never discussed anything with him, but everybody else knew it because I told people I was breeding to sell horned breeding bulls."

"Please look at those cattle yonder. Do you see any with horns?"

"Most of them have horns."

"Do you see any that look to you to have Shorthorn blood in them?"

"Most of them have Shorthorn blood in them."

Spicer said angrily, "I wonder where this is supposed to lead us. Does counsel imply that General Hethcutt has rustled the plaintiff's cattle?"

"I am not implying anything—yet," said Pegram. "I will now ask the witness what is the purpose of this pair of instruments, a blowtorch and a short branding iron that makes only a tiny check mark."

Whiting said, "When I got to where I couldn't afford to hire a man, when I had to send my own daughter to her mother's family in San Francisco, I had to figure out a way, a one-man way, to track my disappearing cattle. I was a soldier most of my life, and I still can't handle a full-grown critter on a rope by myself. Not many men can.

"But I could handle unweaned calves, and I got better and better at it. I couldn't build a fire and risk calling attention to myself by putting my brand on a calf I saw with a cow that wore my brand. I say right here and now

I would have been a dead man if I had tried that, me against this whole Bar H outfit.

"But I could get a rope around a calf's leg and throw it, and sit on its head while I heated up this little iron with my blowtorch. I put the check mark where it wouldn't be easy to see, usually between the hind legs on a female critter, and inside one of the front legs of a bull calf.

"It was a hell of a way to have to do things. My own cows, with my own high-grade Shorthorn calves, and all I could do was try to put a secret mark on them that no-body would see unless he knew where to look for it. Or if somebody happened to see it, it might pass for a wound of some kind. But that's the only way I could mark my calf crop, and I've kept a tally book in code, and it shows that in less than five years, I marked four hundred and fifty-two critters that way."

"Do you have that tally book with you?"

"Yes, I do."

"I ask that it be admitted into evidence as Plaintiff's Exhibit Three."

"Object, object, object to any of these three objects going into the evidence," Spicer exploded. "What do they mean? What can they prove?"

"We won't know that," said Pegram, "until we see if we can find any check marks on the cattle held in this pasture. There is no way we or anyone else could have applied such a mark recently. There is no way it could have been erased or extinguished, once it was burned in. I ask the court to examine these three exhibits carefully, and then rule on their relevancy."

The judge dismounted from the staid old horse that had stood so quietly. He gave scant attention to the blow-torch. He examined the well-worn check-mark branding iron more carefully. He opened the worn old tally book, and frowned.

"Obviously this is a code, and it means nothing unless we have the key to it. I assume you're going to give us that, Mr. Pegram. If you do, I want to know why the plaintiff kept it in code instead of in plain figures."

Whiting explained the simple PINK FLOWER code. "I used it because most of the time I was batching it, living alone, and the farther I got into this, the more I realized I was surrounded by enemies. What if I was found dead with this on me? Why, it would have been thrown in the nearest fire, that's why. This way, there was a chance maybe somebody would save it for a keepsake for my daughter without realizing what it was.

"Look, two years ago, your honor, here's fifteen days when there's not a mark made. That was when I went to San Francisco to testify in a lawsuit. Here's the week of Christmas before last, when my daughter was here. I took time off to be with her. Then there were a couple of times I had sick spells and missed a day or two. I've got witnesses that can prove I was sick because they saw me then."

Hewitt was watching Hethcutt carefully. The man had spent a lifetime cultivating an expressionless face, but he was badly shaken now and it showed on him. He was pallid under his tan, whether from fear or fury, or a combination of both, it was impossible to tell.

He sat there, erect in the saddle, as though reviewing his brigade as it marched past him in double time, his jaw set, his eyes stony. The lawyers argued. To Hewitt, it was clear that the judge was impressed by Alf Whiting's long, patient, and very ingenious plan to find out what was happening to his Shorthorn cattle—and he was not impressed by the overbearing little general.

This did not mean that the judge would be bound by what they learned when they examined these steers. It depended on many things, one being how many check marks they found. Deep in every judge's heart was the ambition to make one ruling in his career that thereafter would be cited as brilliant, decisive, discriminating law. Long after a judge was dead, such a ruling would keep his memory green among the people who counted—other lawyers.

Here was Judge Towers' chance to go down in juridical history, but he would be very careful about it. Very *sure*. He certainly did not want to go into the legal records as the jackass who made one of the worst mistakes ever made on the bench.

"The exhibits will be admitted," Judge Towers said, cutting short the heated debate between the two lawyers. "Now, how do you propose to examine all these critters?"

Pegram deferred to Whiting, who said, "Yonder is a counting chute into a feed lot. It already has a gate in it. Herd these critters through there and stop them long enough for me to look for my secret mark, that's all."

"I'll be damned if you're going to run the flesh off my cattle on any such fool stunt as this," said Hethcutt, unable to contain his anger any longer. "I won't put up with it."

"Your honor," said Pegram, "defendant has already accepted the offer of proof, and this is part of it. If he refuses to go through with it, I will then want to introduce another exhibit. In the past two weeks, my client and his men have secretly roped and inspected certain Bar H cattle. I will ask that the record of these inspections be made part of the evidence and I will then move that the ratio of check-marked cattle found in them be applied to every head of cattle owned by the defendant."

On and on, and finally Spicer had to get his client aside and plead with him to go through with it. Hewitt could see the general's eyes rolling wildly. He could see the jaw muscles twitch as he clenched his teeth. They kept on twitching after he stopped clenching his teeth, when he gave up.

———————◆———————

With both crews working, it went fast. The first critter into the chute was a big red steer, a three-year-old, wild as a deer. He had the curved, short horns of the Shorthorn breed, the squarish face, and the blocky body.

Whiting knelt just outside the chute and felt the steer's pelt just behind the brisket and on the inner side of both legs. He turned and nodded to the judge.

"Here's one," he said.

The judge got down to feel the scar himself. He measured it with his fingers and then measured his fingers against the cold check-mark branding iron.

"Do you wish to challenge this, Mr. Spicer?" he said, while still on his knees. "I believe it would be in your own best interests to do so."

Spicer got down on his knees and let Whiting show him how to find the brand. "I can feel something, all right," Spicer said, "but I can't say it's a check mark and I don't like to be asked to believe what I can feel and not see."

The judge stood up and dusted off his hands. "The court orders that this steer be roped and taken out of the chute, and then thrown and tied so we can make visual verification," he said.

General Hethcutt had regained control of his emotions. He merely sat his horse sternly as a man got a rope around the steer's horns and dragged him through the gate while others held back the rest of the herd. It took three men and three ropes to throw him and hold him.

And there it was, a permanent scar where hair would never grow again. The judge himself fitted the cold branding iron to it, to show how neatly it fit. He looked at Whiting.

"Was this critter an unbranded calf following a cow branded with your brand, Mr. Whiting?" he asked.

"Yes, sir," said Whiting. "Naturally I don't remember him, but if he's got that mark on him, he was sucking one of my branded cows. But you'll notice that he's got a Bar H on his hip, too, put on later."

"This proves nothing," Spicer snapped. "That brand could have been applied at any time up to a year ago."

"By one man?" Whiting asked. "A year ago he would have weighed five or six hundred pounds. That's a big steer. I didn't have any help a year ago, or for a long time before that."

"We will merely record that he bears two brands—a check mark high up inside his left leg, near the brisket, and a Bar H on his hip," the judge said. "Now try another one."

The next one was younger and smaller, but he showed even more evidence of good Shorthorn blood. He was red on top, roan on the sides, mostly white on the belly.

And he had a check-mark brand between his front legs.

He was run on through into the feed lot, and another one, also partly a roan, was roped around the horns and held motionless with his head against the gatepost. Whiting knelt down and felt between his forelegs and then motioned to the judge.

"Another one, your honor. Maybe the general would like to inspect this himself."

General Hethcutt ignored him. The judge made another mark on his paper. Another steer was roped and examined, *and another check mark found on him*. Three in a row. The next one had no check mark, nor did the fifth one.

But the sixth one did, and the eighth and ninth, and then the eleventh, fourteenth, sixteenth, and twentieth. The work was going faster now. No one thought of stopping to eat. They worked straight on through the afternoon and until almost dark before the last steer went through the chute.

"Six hundred and twenty-six head altogether, I make it," the judge announced then, "and two hundred and thirteen are check-marked. That's close to thirty-four per cent."

"I have it on good authority that the Bar H now has more than ten times as many cattle as there are here—about sixty-two hundred and fifty head. If we apply that same percentage to that figure, we will find that two thousand, one hundred and twenty-five of them are check-marked, and therefore the property of my client, Alfred Whiting. And if we—"

"That is a goddamn lie!" the general shouted. "His own tally book only shows four hundred and fifty-two that he check-marked."

"Oh yes," replied Pegram, "but we have never said, never believed, that he branded every one of his calves. It was physically impossible. When I say they are all check-marked, I mean that they are good Shorthorn blood, born to Flying W cows, and bearing the invisible mark of a man who, although alone and defenseless, refused to be victimized by a rustler and a thief."

Somebody leaped to catch the general's arm before he could get his gun out. Hewitt had been watching Crazy Ozzie Hyde, and keeping his own hand close to his gun. He saw Hyde turn to look at him. Their eyes met.

Then the general stopped struggling and Hyde carefully put his right hand on his saddle horn. Hippo Thompson bent his thick leg to help the judge step up into his saddle again.

"I suppose you have some law citations you wish to give me, Mr. Pegram," he said.

"Yes, sir, with copies for Mr. Spicer."

"How about you, Mr. Spicer? Do you have any case law you think the court should consult?"

"No. Not yet, anyway. Who the hell—excuse that, your honor—who in the world would expect a serious claim to arise out of anything as—as silly as this? The California law on livestock brands is old and well established, and every point in it has already been adjudicated."

"Not every point," said Pegram. "We are now adjudicating still another one."

"Very well," said the judge. "I will take this under submission and hear further argument on it one week from today, in court. Court is adjourned for the day."

———◆———

It was the Whiting crew that escorted the judge back to the county road that led to the historic highway El Camino Real, the "King's Highway," first marked by the Franciscans on the northward march from San Diego. Here the judge turned south toward San Luis Obispo, but he would stop for a few days with a rancher friend along the way.

Whiting said not a word, except for a gruff farewell that accompanied his handshake when Tom Pegram took the road to Three Oaks. He looked drawn, tired, and old, like a man who had staked everything on the last big effort of his life. Part of it, Hewitt knew, was the subconscious intimidation of bucking a brigadier general. It took a long time to get that out of your bones, and Whiting still felt the pressure of rank.

What worried Hewitt was Bella. They had left her at home, with the oldest of the cowboys that Hippo had recruited. With Lon Tsan in the area, anything could happen.

It was a relief to see her sitting beside the back door of the house, a big pail of water on the fire she had built, scalding a couple of old hens for tomorrow's supper. She was dressed like a ragamuffin in worn, tight Levi's and a red-checked shirt that also was too tight. Her hair was caught up in a red bandanna and she was barefoot.

She grinned at them. "Why are you all so serious-looking?" she asked, gaily. "Wasn't Uncle Lionel hospitable to you?"

Whiting's first smile of the day creased his face as he got off and handed his reins to one of the men to take care of his horse. Bella stood up to kiss him on the cheek. He gave her a hug that lifted her off her feet.

"If that was hospitality," he said, "I'd rather be run off the place at gunpoint."

"How did the case go?"

He shook his head. "I'm too wound up in it, honey. I'm betting my eating money on one turn of the cards, and you better ask Mr. Hewitt what he thinks."

The girl looked at Hewitt, who did not want to say too much in front of the men. "I think we got all we could possibly expect today," he said. "We go back into court a week from today, after the judge has had time to study the evidence. There's only one thing that worries me."

"What's that?"

"He's got to try Rex Patterson's suit next, without the check marks for evidence I wonder how he's going to feel about making a ruling in your father's case that would have to apply to Patterson's."

"Well, I don't know how lawyers think—" the girl started to say.

Her father interrupted her. "Nobody does."

"Well, then, I just bet you anything that he'll pick Uncle Lionel like I'm picking these hens. Rustling is still rustling and we all thought those days were gone forever."

"Still, a brigadier general—"

"Retired, Dad," she reminded him, "and the judge isn't retired, and I'll bet Uncle Lionel acted like he was commanding a brigade and the judge was just a damn-fool civilian."

She was a smart little devil, Hewitt thought. Before he headed for the bunkhouse with the men, he saw Sneaky plodding like a tame old house cat down the slope through the trees. Hippo Thompson saw him, too, and his hand dropped to his gun. He never had gotten used to a male lion big enough to be a potential killer having the run of the place.

They all had a drink for good luck before sitting down to beefsteak and potatoes fried with onions. Something put them all in a jovial mood. Whiting was relaxed for the first time today—in several days, Hewitt saw now. They jammed the tiny kitchen from wall to wall, filling the plank table that Whiting had enlarged for his enlarged crew.

As the men streamed out afterward in the dusk, Lon Tsan came quietly and inconspicuously down the slope from the secret little hut they had built for him. Whiting had dozed off in his old rocking chair.

"Don't wake him. It's you I would like to talk to, Mr. Hewitt," Lon Tsan said.

They sat down on the woodpile behind the kitchen, and Lon Tsan asked what had happened at the Bar H.

What he told Lon Tsan would be repeated in a day or two to Giacomo Gabrielini. He recounted the facts and watched Lon Tsan write down the figures.

"You think Alf has a chance to win his case, Mr. Hewitt?"

"A very good chance, I would say. If the judge is a mathematician, and if he computes the losses year by year, he may reduce the award to Alf by quite a bit. But Alf has asked for punitive damages, too, and I think if the judge holds that Hethcutt stole those cattle, he's going to give him hell."

Lon Tsan seemed satisfied. As they stood up, Hewitt offered his hand first. Lon Tsan shook it firmly.

"Prayers are in order at this point, I think," he said. "Now we need all the help we can get."

Hewitt smiled. "Yes, you pray to your God and we'll pray to ours."

"An avalanche starts with a single clod. That is a good thing to keep in mind. Good-bye, Mr. Hewitt."

He walked away through the trees. Hewitt felt sure he would not walk all the way to San Francisco this time.

Darkness fell as Hewitt sat there smoking a cigar and relaxing after one of the most unusual days he had ever spent. In a moment he saw Sneaky slinking toward him, and he could not help but flinch a little. The big cat only wanted some loving, however. He leaned against Hewitt and demanded to have his belly and back scratched.

A few minutes later, Bella appeared. She was drying her hair with a big, heavy towel, and she smelled of soap. She had put on fresh clothing and obviously was just out of the bath. She sat down on the ground in front of him and a little below him.

"Help dry my hair," she said.

"I'm afraid I wouldn't be very good at that. I've never

done it before," he replied. Despite himself he felt his heart beating a little faster.

"There's a first time for everything. It's such a damned nuisance, why can't you be nice and help?"

"All right, all right."

He took the towel and began squeezing her heavy hair in it. She leaned back and put her upper arms across his legs, bowing her head forward so he could manipulate her hair. His heart went on thudding, but he went on puffing his cigar, too, stopping now and then to dust off the ashes.

"Throw that thing away," she said suddenly.

It was about gone anyway. He put it down and ground it out under his heel, gouging a pit in the dirt next to her hip and then grinding the cigar until no spark remained. The girl reached up and ran her hands through her hair.

"That's as dry as it's going to get unless I get a dry towel," she whispered.

He folded the towel and handed it to her. "I think you're right."

She leaned back against him and parted her hair so that it fell across her shoulders and over her bosom. She looked up at him, her face pale and lovely in the dark, her lips parted.

"Kiss me," she whispered.

"Now you're being downright foolish, Bella."

"Why?"

"You're even more foolish to ask that. I'm not in love with you, I'm old enough to be your father, I'm your father's friend, and I'm not a marrying man."

"Oh, pooh!"

She reached up and caught at his hair, knocking his hat off in the process. She pulled his face down until his lips were pressing on hers—hard. He felt the tip of her tongue tantalizing his mouth.

He gathered her into his arms and kissed her fiercely. She gave a little whimper and tried to squirm into his lap. He let go of her suddenly and then, as she fell, caught her face between his hands. He made himself smile.

"All right, your little experiment is over, Bella," he said. "You're a very desirable girl—"

"Woman," she corrected him.

"Very well, a very desirable woman, but I'm not what you want and you're not what I need. So we're not going to get into this situation again, are we?"

He slapped her across the bottom. "Damn!" she said, as she stood up. She put her hands on her hips and glowered down at him.

"Hewitt, nothing would make Daddy any happier than for us to get married," she said.

"Has he said so?"

"Yes."

"And you regard that as permission to seduce me?"

"Yes. How do you think my mother got Daddy?"

"I thought it was the other way round. I thought he tolled her off for an illicit week and didn't bring her back until it was too late to salvage their reputations."

"What nonsense! Mama always was determined to marry a *forestiero*, if you know what that means."

"I know. A foreigner, a non-Italian."

"Yes. They had a nice, rich, fat boy picked out for her by the time she was twelve. She picked on Daddy as the one man dumb enough to risk making the whole family mad. It's bad enough to seduce an Italian woman today—it was a hundred times worse then. But Daddy made them respect him. They voted to let them get married. Can you imagine it? The family *voted* on it! And he made her happy. At first she was just using him but by the time they got back, my mother was really and truly in love with him."

"How do you know so much about it?"

"I've been told about it often enough. Some of the old folks still hold it against Daddy and me. But times are changing fast, Hewitt. We—"

"By the way, brat, if you can't call me 'Mister' Hewitt, at least call me by my first name."

She studied him a moment. Sneaky got up and went over to lean against her legs. She scratched him behind the ears and made him purr like a broken-down steam engine.

"You know what I like most about you?" she asked.

"No, and I'm afraid to ask," he said.

"You really are a bastard, you know," she said. She turned and went slowly back to the house, hips swaying, the towel bunched in her hand. He had a feeling that somehow he had come out second best this time.

Chapter Seven

The mail rider who made a twice-weekly trip to Paso Robles to serve several ranches and the town of Three Oaks the next day brought Hewitt a letter from his partner. Conrad Meuse was discreet to the point of unintelligibility sometimes, but it paid. They had had several letters intercepted and both had learned to write in a sort of code:

J. Hewitt, Esq.

Subject graduated in bottom 10th of class at WP. 2L 2 mo, then inactive. Took job Baltmerc meanwhile lobbying permstat. Active duty 13 mo later, Dakter. Baltmerc sold out compet fol year short 5 and 4 Z's. Unable fix blame. Subject rated "ad" in staff. No line duty until 1L 3 yrs ltr. CoComan killed action, temp CC, then promot capt & back to staff.

No friends I can determine. No serious blems on rec. As LC svd against Chir w/o distinction. 2 yrs Wash col, staff duty, then command braggart. Told by outspoken foe was offered star to retire.

Hear several bad investments but no details. Once rep engaged wealthy Eng dip dtr but she was sped home. Also hear duel challenge hushed up twice. Sum up: Bad judgment, wants wealth, vicious temper, no scruples, but never antag hibrass. Family BG nil, father street RR promoter, bankrupt, mother ran off with man when subject ten. Something wrong with subject, urge extreme caution always.

C.M.

Reading between the lines, Hewitt learned that brevet Brigadier General Hethcutt had been a poor cadet at West Point and was not commissioned. Worked for a Baltimore mercantile house while lobbying for a commission, which he got thirteen months later. In the following year the Baltimore wholesaler had to sell out to a competitor because it was short $50,000 in its books.

Hethcutt never got better than an "adequate" rating as a staff officer. Assigned to field duty, he was quickly replaced after his captain was killed in action, and then went back to staff duty. Had no personal friends in the Army but nothing seriously wrong with his record. As lieutenant colonel he had commanded troops against the Chiricahua Apaches but soon found himself back on staff duty in Washington. For a while he was commanding officer at Fort Bragg and the gossip was he had been offered his brevet brigadier's star to retire.

His reputation as a speculator was already known to Hewitt, but the effort to marry a wealthy English heiress was news. So was the report that he had twice let his unreliable temper get away from him to the point where he challenged other officers to pistol duels. Otherwise, although a bad officer, he had never done anything to antagonize the high brass, probably because he was a fawning subordinate if a fiery martinet to the men he commanded.

There were officers like that, and too many survived to retire honorably. How a youth with Hethcutt's squalid family background had gotten into West Point in the first place was always politics. Maybe some congressman had been mixed up in a little street-railway promotion himself, and had bought his way out of trouble by nominating young Lionel Hethcutt to the Point.

One thing was sure—if Conrad Meuse urged extreme caution because there was "something wrong" with Hethcutt, he needed watching. Hewitt caught the train to San Francisco and, from a good hotel, sent Giacomo Gabrielini a note asking for a private meeting.

He was surprised and dismayed to get a reply suggesting a rather popular Italian restaurant that was always crowded, but the moment he stepped inside the door he was recognized and conducted through the dining room to the kitchen. Off the kitchen was a small, private dining room where a feast had already been laid out. The banker had had trouble restraining himself until Hewitt got there. He sent the waiter away and himself opened the wine bottles.

"No business until we have eaten a little! We have our own tiny shrimp in San Francisco Bay, and Arturo has a sauce for them that is indescribable. Here, tuck this around you," he said, handing Hewitt a napkin the size of a small tablecloth.

The wine was excellent, the shrimp so delicious that Hewitt followed the banker's example and ate them with a soup spoon. Next came chicken and veal cooked together, with a different wine on the side. And with each dish there was a different pasta, and in the center of the table a huge, circular tray of antipasto, several meals in itself.

I had better close this out fast, Hewitt thought, before this man eats himself to death. . . . He let himself go and enjoyed more food than he usually ate, but when the huge *torta di mele* was served, with a dish of clotted cream to pile on it, Gabrielini had eaten three times as much as he.

"So!" the banker said, as he attacked the apple tart and cream. "The lowly sergeant had the patience to spread his deadly traps for five years, did he? And caught himself a general!"

"He hasn't caught him yet. The judge still has to rule," said Hewitt.

"He will rule in Alf Whiting's favor, my attorneys tell me."

"I hope so, but when you assail the sanctity of livestock brands—"

"This suit assails only an individual. Really, my dear Hewitt, it supports the sanctity of brands."

"I feel so myself, and I only hope the judge sees it that way. If Hethcutt loses, he'll appeal, of course."

"Whiting is a patient man. He can wait. I cannot. I assume you have made no progress on finding my bank's missing money?"

"I haven't even looked for it. One thing at a time. I have had another letter from my partner. It doesn't tell us much that we didn't already know. But it does warn that we're dealing with a real bastard in Hethcutt, a dangerous man with an unreliable temper, a bad man to push into a corner."

"Does Conrad say anything about where he might have secreted the loot from this deal of mine?"

"No. This is background material that only warns us to expect the worst."

Gabrielini finished his portion of *torta* and helped himself to some more. "My auditors and investigators have been busy. We cannot trace one cent of the money to any kind of investment. He either invested it abroad—"

"Not likely, in my estimation," Hewitt cut in. "He'll

want it where he can get his hands on it. One delicate matter—are you sure the Taorellis are innocent? That has been troubling me."

"They lost heavily, too. I have been able to prove that."

"When did Hethcutt's wife last visit her family?"

"Perhaps two years ago."

"Do you think they're estranged?"

Gabrielini shrugged. "Who knows? The family does not talk about its private affairs. My impression is that they feel they have two dead daughters, Zoe and Bernardina. That she is lost to them forever."

"Is she that much in love with Hethcutt?"

Again Gabrielini shrugged. "Who knows? I have had reports from detectives who interviewed men who have worked for the Bar H. There is a possibility that she is a captive, a willing one who can't face the world after what she has done to her family, but who has nothing to do with her husband. I don't know how reliable this information is."

Hewitt said slowly, "First we've got to get the cattle business on its way. Push hard on that and see what reaction we get out of the general. When it comes to the big money he absconded with, I studied him pretty well and I think he's the kind who would want it near to hand. Negotiable and easy to grab and run with. I'm thinking in terms of diamonds, for instance. They're a favorite means of reducing illegal funds to pocket size."

Gabrielini shook his head. "I thought of that, too. Had there been any substantial purchase of diamonds, I would have heard of it by now because I looked for it in the right places. You can confirm that by asking Lon Tsan."

"Gold?"

"Gold is always good, but unless it is coinage it is not

easily disposed of. Illegal deals in bullion always require a discount of up to fifty per cent."

"You've been paying Bernardina what purports to be the income from the trust fund?"

"Yes, and Bella, too. And it can't go on forever. I have put up fifty thousand from my own funds to cover these payments so the bank will not suffer."

"How much per year do these two get?"

"About eleven hundred dollars each."

"Do you know what Bella does with hers?"

"It is all deposited back in the bank in a personal savings account."

"Does her father know about it?"

"I'm sure he does. The last I looked, she had a little over six thousand dollars in the account. The impression I get of the man, he wouldn't touch his own daughter's money."

Gabrielini cocked his head. With a twinkle in his eye, he went on, "How is Bella, by the way?"

"Fine. The ranch life and hard work seem to suit her."

"I thought perhaps you had made a conquest there, friend Hewitt."

Lon Tsan had been talking too much. "Well, you know how impressionable young girls are."

"No, really, I don't. How are they?"

"Impressionable."

The banker laughed a booming laugh. "Well, we have exchanged information, and what have we gained? Exactly nothing that we did not know before. Or am I wrong? You seem to be brooding about something."

"I wish I had the opportunity to search Hethcutt's house thoroughly, before he had a chance to move anything."

"You think the loot is there?"

"It's the most logical conclusion. It fits the man's mentality and personality."

"To have it handy to his hand. In what form?"

"Currency," said Hewitt.

"My God, what a risk that would be! Suppose the house caught fire? Currency is only paper."

"Not if it's secreted in a safe or well insulated from heat and flames."

Gabrielini was silent a moment, studying Hewitt. "Have you ever had a case like this before?"

"No two cases are alike, but yes, I have had others that taught me a few things that may apply here. I want to get some sleep so I can catch the southbound train. Have you arranged to be informed of the judge's action next week?"

"Certainly. An early jolly day is in prospect for some unfortunate men who rely on the pipe. One thing I should like to ask you. Lon Tsan says there is a mountain lion that joins them in the smoking room, and has become addicted. Is this possible?"

"Not just possible. It's a fact."

"He runs free around the place? Bella is exposed to that danger daily?"

"He's not dangerous. I don't know what he would be if he lost the solace of opium for a couple of weeks, but as long as he's dependent on human beings for his pipe, he's a pussycat."

"You have personally seen him?"

"I scratch his ears and belly with these hands two or three times a day."

"My God! What a dangerous life you lead, between that puma and Bella."

Hewitt reached for a cigar to cover his momentary amused confusion. "I've been in worse situations. One more thing—I want to draw on you for more cash to hire more riders. I want to be just a little stronger in man-power than Hethcutt when the showdown comes, and we've got a man who can find them."

"How much do you want, and in what form?"

"Two thousand, in currency, nothing bigger than a ten."

The banker stood up. "Come, let's go get it. You know, Hewitt, at times I envy you. Talking to Conrad I get the impression that you live a lusty, adventurous life that never gets boring. But I think I would rather be bored than be forced to associate on intimate terms with a full-grown mountain lion."

"Believe me," said Hewitt, "Bella is the greater danger of the two."

———◆———

The moment he got back to the Flying W, he cornered Alf Whiting. "Alf," he said, "our problem now is man-power. We need to hire men."

As usual, Whiting's granite face did not change, but Hewitt knew it hurt him to say, "I'm broke. You know that."

"Part of our normal expenses. My firm will foot the bill. It's not the first time we have speculated this way and it won't be the last."

"Mr. Hewitt, you're in charge. If you back me with your own money, you must feel pretty sure of winning this damn case. I feel better," said Whiting.

Hewitt sent Hippo out that very night, and again Hippo circled the Bar H and headed for the San Joaquin Valley. He returned in five days with nine extremely com-petent-looking men. They were not, Hewitt decided, the kind of men to whom you would introduce your only sister.

But in a tight spot, when you needed tough, faithful

men at your back, these were the ones you would want. Hippo also had brought a cook.

"I know you didn't say nothing about that, Jeff," he said, "but Miss Whiting already has more than she can do, and this fellow's good. There's lumber enough around here that we can run up a kitchen, dining room, and bigger bunkhouse in a few days."

"It's something I should have thought of, Hippo, and I appreciate it," Hewitt said. "I hope you explained to these fellows about Sneaky."

"Yes, and they don't exactly like it, but between us, we ought to be able to show that he's just a tame old house cat."

He hesitated. "I had to tell them about Lon Tsan, too," he went on. "That don't bother them half as much as that damn lion."

The puma's appearance that evening kept the new men on edge. Sneaky himself was on edge. It was almost time for his pipe, and he kept rubbing against the strangers, coaxing them to give him what he needed. You had to hand it to them, the way they kept their nerves with at least a hundred and fifty pounds of killer cat coaxing them for attention.

The cook was a tough little old man with a short leg. He set up his stove in the open and let them build the kitchen around him, and until the dining room would be finished, fed the men in the open too. Bella came up to where Hewitt was standing, watching the crew swarm over the building they were framing.

"Where will you eat?" she demanded.

"Why, I've usually found it a good practice to chow with my men," Hewitt replied.

She gave him a sullen look. "But Dad will eat in the house with me, I suppose."

"That's up to him, but he probably will."

"Then so will you. You're a boss, not a hired hand."

"That thought had occurred to me, too," he said, "but I'll probably bunk with the men."

Unexpectedly her face cleared and became positively radiant as she smiled. Sneaky came up then, and pushed between them. The cat probably had saved him some further embarrassment, Hewitt thought.

Lon Tsan appeared that night, and Sneaky vanished up the slope to the grotto in the hillside. In the morning, Hewitt saw Lon Tsan mount a fine horse and ride down toward the highway. The cat did not stagger out into the open until close to noon, and then he curled up near the house and dozed contentedly.

They finished roofing the bunkhouse and kitchen the night before they were due in court in San Luis Obispo. They were tired, but they were on the road early the next morning. They were ahead of the Bar H crew, they saw, when they tied up in the town wagon lot behind the courthouse.

Tom Pegram was waiting for them in the empty courtroom. He was not overconfident, but neither was he nervous. "When you have done the best you can with what you feel is a good case, all you can get is old by fussing about it," he said.

Hewitt grinned at him. "I've had the same feeling myself a few times."

From the window of the courthouse they saw General Hethcutt ride into town at the head of his column of men —and that's what they were, a column, twenty-two strong, strung out like rookie cavalrymen. They filed into the courthouse in the same military order, led by the strutting general.

Long before the time for court to open, every seat in

the courtroom was filled, and a crowd jammed the hallway outside. Again the young deputy went through the crowd, collecting belted guns, and this time he had another man to help him carry them. And again the sheriff was home, ill.

There was that period, no more than two or three minutes, just before court opened, when Hewitt became aware of a heightened tension in the crowd. People shot to their feet when ordered to rise for the judge's entrance, sat down as quietly as possible when told to.

The judge took his place at the bench. "Do either of you desire to make a motion before I address myself to the offer of proof already made and accepted?" he asked.

Both attorneys arose. "If it please the court," Pegram said, "I should like to reserve any such motion until we have heard from the court." Spicer could barely wait until Pegram had sat down. "At this time," he said, "I wish to reject the so-called offer of proof and I move that it be stricken from the record."

"Denied" was all the judge said.

He picked up a sheaf of papers. Hewitt, sitting in the audience behind Pegram and Whiting, kept a sharp eye on General Hethcutt. He could see him only in profile, but his face was fiery red, his lips were curled under his big mustache, and it seemed to Hewitt that he was keeping his emotions under a very tight rein indeed. He was used to exploding in a temper tantrum whenever he felt like it, and to be outranked by a mere civilian was almost more than he could take.

"In the first place," the judge went on, in a flat, steady, but carrying voice, "I am going to accept the check-mark device as valid evidence. . . . No, Mr. Spicer, if you have an objection to that you may make it later. Please have the courtesy to sit down and listen.

"The court takes due notice of the fact that we have only plaintiff's word and the log he alleged he kept in code to back up his claim that he applied the check mark only to calves following cows marked with his own Flying W brand. But in support of such claim, the court also takes cognizance of the great preponderance of Shorthorn blood in the Bar H herd. In plaintiff's brief, attention is called to the fact that he bought one dozen good Shorthorn bulls and that defendant never owned any. In his demurrer, defendant ignored this point altogether.

"I have tried many cases about cattle, and have familiarized myself with the characteristics of the various breeds, and the way they are carried from generation to generation. I believe that any old cattleman inspecting that herd would have counted fifty per cent of them to be half Shorthorn, twenty-five per cent of them to be one fourth Shorthorn, and twenty-five of them to be three fourths Shorthorn. I kept notes and that is my own appraisal.

"I conclude that plaintiff has been systematically victimized by the theft of his best calves for a long time, and I need not speculate on how or why it happened that they ended up in the Bar H herds. All I must determine now is the extent of the damage to plaintiff. I now hand each of you a set of mathematical calculations by which I arrived at a conclusion."

He leaned across the bench holding two sheaves of yellow foolscap. Hewitt glanced at Tom Pegram and saw the bewilderment on his face as he looked at the three pages. General Hethcutt stood up to look at them with Spicer. He was goggle-eyed with incredulous shock and surprise, and he could not keep his mouth shut.

"Is this Boolean algebra?" he said, looking up at the judge. His voice was almost a snarl.

"Yes, it is," said the judge. "Are you familiar with it?"

"More or less. But this is beyond me, and I never heard of it in a court of law before."

"Neither have I, your honor," said Tom Pegram. "I beg the court's enlightenment."

"Boolean algebra," said the judge, "is an old hobby of mine. It is a system of mathematics by which problems in nonmathematical logic can be solved by applying the laws of algebra to them. It was formulated by George Boole, one of the world's foremost mathematicians, who died in 1864 in his native England.

"I do not expect you to understand these equations, gentlemen, but if you take an appeal, and the higher court consults with the best mathematicians in the world, I assure you they will stand up. I am in constant correspondence with mathematicians all over the world, and myself have contributed no little bit to our understanding of Boole's methods. In any case, there are my findings."

"If it please the court," said Pegram, with a small, rueful grin, "they leave me right where I was in the beginning."

"Because they only show the *method* by which I reached the decision on the damages. Based on those equations, I now find that plaintiff has suffered the theft of two thousand, eight hundred and sixty-one calves over the period he was trying to breed up a Shorthorn herd. They were always his best calves, and under time-honored precedent, we must value them at their fair market value *as adult animals*. You will note that page three analyzes the prices on the cattle market for the past ten years.

"There we find that a beef animal of good quality *averaged* eighteen dollars and ninety-three cents. Simple multiplication shows us that plaintiff therefore was robbed of cattle worth fifty-four thousand, one hundred and fifty-eight dollars and seventy-three cents. The court herewith awards that amount in real damages, plus punitive damages in the amount of twenty thousand, eight hundred and forty-one dollars and twenty-seven cents, for a total of seventy-five thousand dollars.

"I will now hear any motions counsel may wish to make."

Hewitt had been following the judge's slow, level speech with increasing excitement, and perhaps as much incredulity as the general. He was quick with figures, and he had had Boolean algebra explained to him a few times —enough to make a believer of him. It would never have occurred to him to consult a Boolean mathematician in this case, but what luck to find a country judge who had it at his command!

Hethcutt, still standing beside his lawyer, yanked the three pages of foolscap out of the lawyer's hand and crumpled them in his fist. His mouth worked silently. Suddenly it burst from him, out of control.

"This is a goddamn outrage," he shouted. "You accuse me of being a cattle rustler—I, who fought the Indians and retired honorably as a brigadier general. You use this —this mystical *shit* now to try to rob an old soldier of his property—"

Spicer was trying to get him to sit down, but big as he was and small as Hethcutt was beside him, the tough little general kept his feet and kept brandishing the wadded foolscap at the court.

"We'll see who carries the heaviest guns in his train," he shouted. "Any time a hick judge can sit here in a country courthouse and rob a retired general of a fortune, all I can say is that this country has gone completely to hell.

I'll carry this all the way to the Supreme Court, by Christ, and get you laughed off the goddamn bench."

Spicer finally forced the general to sit down. Once he was off his feet, Hethcutt seemed to lose the power of speech. He took his handkerchief out with trembling hands and wiped his face with it. The judge held up his hands to silence Spicer.

"I am going to hold you in contempt of court for that outburst, Mr. Hethcutt," he said. "I am going to fine you one hundred dollars and sentence you to one day in jail. If you so much as open your mouth in this courtroom again, without first receiving my permission *through your attorney*, I will regard it as an additional offense and deal with you accordingly."

He looked at Tom Pegram. Pegram was still somewhat dazed, but he could think on his feet. "Mr. Pegram," said the judge, "have you any motions to make at this time?"

"No, and it please the court," Pegram said. "My only comment would be an expression of gratitude for a learned and wise judgment that redresses the grievances of my client."

The judge looked at Spicer. "Have you any motions, sir?"

"I move for a new trial."

"Denied."

"I request thirty days in which to appeal."

"Granted, but I want it understood that this defendant is not to move any cash or other property out of the jurisdiction of this court in that time."

"Thank you, your honor. I must at this time request that the sentence of contempt be expunged from the record. Only the sentence, sir! My client was, unfortunately, in contempt of the court. But I cannot see how the court can confine a retired brigadier general to serve even one day in jail when—"

"Denied," the judge cut in. He glanced at the courtroom clock. "It is now seven minutes after eleven. The sheriff will take custody of Lionel Hethcutt and confine him to a cell in the jail until seven minutes after eleven tomorrow morning. And while we're playing military marches, I may say that it ill becomes a general, even one of mere brevet rank, to rob a sergeant who also had a long and honorable career.

"You see, counselor, I served in the Army against the Apaches, too. I was an enlisted man in the cavalry and my highest rank was lance corporal. I look back on my service, however, with considerable pride. I might add that my father's brother was a sergeant in the Seventh Cavalry when it was wiped out at the Battle of the Little Big Horn. His body had eight arrows and three bullet holes in it. In short, I'm not a greenhorn when it comes to the military.

"Do not read into my attitude any bias toward the officer corps, whose honor, integrity, and bravery I honor highly. But my court is as sacred to our form of government as civilian control of the military, and no court of appeal would permit me to be bullied by any officer of any rank. We stand in recess."

Hewitt could not believe that it was over, even when he saw the deputy sheriff come into the courtroom from a door behind the bench and put his hand on Hethcutt's shoulder and lead him away through the same door. An old enlisted man himself, Hewitt had never been an enthusiast for military justice. It pleased some part of his soul to learn that even a retired brevet brigadier general could be made subject to something like a summary court-martial.

He signaled the Flying W men to remain seated and let Spicer herd Hethcutt's crew down the aisle and out the public door. He signaled them again—*stay here*—and caught Tom Pegram's arm and hurried him down the aisle after Spicer. They caught the stunned and shaken attorney just outside the door, where he was surrounded by Hethcutt's tough-looking crew.

"Just a moment, Mr. Spicer," he said.

Spicer looked at him dazedly. "Yes?"

"I imagine this is a bitter moment for your client, perhaps for his men, too. I am going to see to it that Alf Whiting's men remain in the courtroom for another ten minutes. Then we will go to our horses and go straight home. We brought grub to eat in the saddle. There is no need for the two crews to meet and perhaps get into a fight."

A wiry, unshaven man with a rat's glittering eyes pushed forward. Crazy Ozzie Hyde could not comprehend anything except that his boss had lost his case in court, and what he did not understand, he hated.

"This don't end it, Hewitt," he said. "You-all can skulk here in the goddamn court as long as you like, but we'll meet again sometime."

"And when we do," Hewitt said, "you want to warn me to draw my gun on sight, is that it?"

"That's it."

"If that happens, I'll kill you. I'll pump three forty-five slugs into you before you fall. You're not a bad man, Hyde. It's just the way your mama combs your hair that makes you look like that."

"You son of a bitch!"

Hyde lunged at Hewitt, but his holster was empty, the

sheriff again having disarmed everyone before allowing them to enter the courtroom. Spicer grabbed at Hyde and got a hold on his shirt and hauled him back. He took two blows in the body before Spicer finally bore him back among his own comrades.

"What are you trying to do, get the general a penitentiary sentence?" he said. "I don't like to be ordered around by this man, Hewitt, either. But either you get out of town immediately, and make no trouble for the Flying W men after you leave town, or General Hethcutt can get another lawyer."

Hewitt saw nothing but enmity in the faces of the Bar H crew, but the starch had gone out of them. The judge's devastating ruling had gone over their heads like a shrieking heavy-caliber bullet. They began filing out, Crazy Ozzie among them. A deputy sheriff gave them back their guns on the steps of the courthouse.

Hewitt returned to the table where Alf Whiting sat with his head in his hands. He did not understand what had happened, either. Hewitt watched the clock tick off a full fifteen minutes, during which Pegram tried to make Whiting see that he had seventy-five thousand dollars coming to him, before tapping him on the shoulder.

"I want to try to see the judge a minute, and ask him for a copy of those equations. Then I think we ought to get home. Bella has a right to know how big you've won," Hewitt said.

Whiting just sat there. His stolid self-control had almost cracked, but no jubilation showed in his face. He motioned for Hewitt to lean down.

"That algebra stuff," he whispered. "How far can they go with it? I mean, suppose I marked a deck here and there in my life, could they go back with that damn stuff and prosecute me?"

Hewitt knew that Alf was worrying about his peculations in disposing of army surplus. "No further back than the statute of limitations, which is four years for everything but murder. There is no statute of limitations on murder."

Whiting slumped, with a great shudder of relief. Hewitt knocked on the door of the judge's chambers, and the judge got up and let him in.

"Excuse me, sir," said Hewitt, "but I wonder if there's an extra copy of those equations that I could have?"

"Oh, are you interested in Boole?"

"He's away over my head, but my partner is a mathematician of sorts. He's a member of some kind of international mathematical society, and swaps problems with people all over the world."

"I'm probably a fellow member. I would be very glad to supply you with a copy. I could let you have an envelope to mail it in. I might mail it myself, if you will permit. I would enjoy corresponding with another mathematician."

Hewitt gave him one of his cards, and the judge, flattered and pleased, promised to get the three sheets of equations off in the next mail. Hewitt left Whiting and the crew waiting at the courthouse while he went to the railway station to send two telegrams. The first was to Conrad, and it said:

WON LAWSUIT BIG STOP IMPORTANT DOCUMENTS COMING BY MAIL STOP URGENT YOU WRITE ME OPINION OF SAME SOONEST STOP

The other wire went to Benhart and Company, San Francisco. It was through this nonexistent firm that Hewitt and Meuse had been exchanging letters and wires with Giacomo Gabrielini for almost a year. This one said:

BIG LEGAL VICTORY STOP IF LOSER OFFERS COMPROMISE
SETTLEMENT HOW MUCH CAN HE RAISE QMK LOTS CAN
BRING REPLY

You had to have a cat at every rat hole. If Conrad
could not evaluate the equations he could quickly forward them to someone who could, and another opinion
might make the difference to an appeals court. As for the
one to the banker, it was important to know how much
General Hethcutt could offer without digging into the
missing bank loot. "Lots," as used in the telegram, meant
Lon Tsan, who was just leaving the depot as Hewitt entered it. They passed without a sign of recognition.

Chapter Eight

On the way home, Hewitt and Whiting rode apart from the crew. They were silent for a long time, as Alf tried to think how to approach Hewitt with the tale of the surplus property.

"Usually an enlisted man thinks he has won the jackpot if he can slip home five pounds of corned beef for his wife to cook," he said.

"How well I know it!" Hewitt replied.

"But if a man is smart and patient and careful, and cuts the right officers in, sometimes he can make some real money."

"Alf, are you trying to tell me about that surplus program? I already know all about it."

"The hell you do!" Whiting hauled in his horse briefly. "How do you know it? Why?"

"Before we undertook your case, we did a pretty thorough investigation of it. Lon Tsan recommended us, didn't he?"

"Yes."

"We're bondsmen for the officers of the Tuscan-American National Bank of San Francisco. That's where he heard of us."

Whiting narrowed his eyes. "Mr. Hewitt, I don't like that a damn bit. My wife was Italian. Them Italian families stick together. For a while it was even money whether they'd let us get married or kill me."

"That's all in the past." Hewitt had to think how to say it, with Whiting in this suspicious, angry mood. "Alf, exactly how much personal contact did you have with Hethcutt in that business with the army surplus?"

"What's that got to do with it?"

"It could be useful information. I like to know everything there is to know about a case I'm on."

But Hewitt knew he was not going to get much from Whiting this day. "I got the enlisted man's dirty end of the stick, that's all. He had the rank to cover both of us, or send me to prison."

"One other thing. How did you meet Lon Tsan?"

"He came to me before I moved onto the ranch and laid his cards on the table. He was after Hethcutt too, over that swindle that wrecked his family. If there's anybody that has more family feeling than an Italian it's a Chinese. If you're a friend to one, you're a friend to all— and nobody ever needed friends worse than I did then. And patient? They can wait years, if they have to! As long as it takes."

Ahead they could see the small flurry of dust where Hethcutt's crew, no doubt with hearts cindery with hatred and frustration, had cut across toward the Bar H. The winter rains now were long past. The range was already brown, and would stay that way until the rains came with the winter again.

That was quite a crew Hethcutt had. Hewitt, looking back over his shoulder at the men Hippo Thompson was leading, felt better to have them on his side. It was a cinch that things would get worse before they got better around here.

They opened a gate, rode through it into the oak-dotted Flying W range, and closed it behind them. An hour later they were approaching the house—no longer a cabin, but a fairly large, comfortable ranch house in which Hewitt had invested a considerable sum of Tuscan-American money. At least now Whiting would be able to pay it back, after he collected from his old enemy.

Bella saw them coming and leaped into the saddle of the horse she had kept waiting. She came racing toward them, wearing Levi's and a shirt, with her hair in twin pigtails.

"Is it over already?" she cried.

"Yes, honey, and we won," her father said.

She brought her horse up close to his and threw her arms around him. "Oh, golly, Dad, how much did we win?"

"Don't go spending it now because they're sure to appeal it and stall forever, but we got a judgment of seventy-five thousand dollars."

"No!" she screamed.

"Ask Mr. Hewitt."

The whole crew pushed up to surround her and enjoy the look of pleasure shining on her pretty face. At this moment it was impossible to think of her as an adult temptress who was deliberately trying to seduce Hewitt. Here was a surprised and delighted kid, that was all.

"Is Daddy telling the truth?" she asked Hewitt.

"He surely is. You're probably going to have a long wait before you get your hands on any cash, but the trial judge handed down a decision that I think is going to be almost impossible to overturn."

"Oh, poor Aunt Bernardina!"

Her face turned woeful. "Why?" Hewitt asked. "They won't be broke. He's a rich man."

"But he'll take it out on her, and her life is already miserable enough."

She said nothing more at the time, but as soon as supper was over, she threw Hewitt a look that ordered him to follow her. He waited at the table in the bunkhouse dining room a moment before ambling outside. He saw her working in the little garden she had started back of the barn.

She leaned on her hoe. "Hewitt, I've got to trust you and ask you to do something for me," she said.

"I'll do anything I can that doesn't get me into trouble with your father," he said.

"It would if he knew about it. I'm not supposed to have anything to do with Aunt Bernardina and she's not supposed to have anything to do with me, but I've met her twice since I've been here."

"How did this happen?"

"We—we've got a signal we use. That's what I want you to do, put up the signal for her to meet me."

"Where?"

"At Three Oaks. Or just outside it."

"Why, Bella?"

"Uncle Lionel is the worst bully in the world, and he'll take it out on her. I want to see her and let her know I still want to be friends with her."

"I'm not sure that's such a good idea, Bella."

"Please?"

"How does she get away to meet you?"

"She has a team and buggy and she often goes just for rides. Anything to get away from there! Please. You can go with me this time."

He gave in because he wanted to meet General Hethcutt's wife himself. She told him how to leave the signal. Early the next morning, he saddled a horse and went for a canter "to enjoy a restful smoke," he said. A few miles up the highway, on the Bar H side of the fence, stood a windmill that fed one big tank. The overflow from that tank fed another, so there were usually dozens of cattle around it.

On the iron frame of the windmill hung several tin cans a man could use to catch a drink with. Most were pretty rusty. He chose the rustiest of all, and bent the top together so it could not be used. On the bottom, he scratched with the point of his pocketknife, "3 P.M. Friday."

That was all it would take, Bella said. Hewitt had tied his horse to the fence to climb through the wire fence, and was uneasy until he was back in the saddle again. He could see for miles, but mostly over what was now definitely enemy territory.

Coming toward him down the road was a slim, strong man with a small pack on his back. Hewitt waited for him. It was Lon Tsan, dressed like a working man, with a battered old hat on his head. Yesterday, gliding unobtrusively around San Luis Obispo, he had worn an inconspicuous gray suit and cap.

Hewitt dismounted to shake hands. "Don't tell me you've been to San Francisco and back!" he said.

The Chinese smiled, and when he did so he looked like a man of fifty-five or sixty years—which he probably was. When his face was sedately composed, as it was most of the time, he looked barely forty.

"No, only Paso Robles," Lon Tsan said. "Our mutual friend spent the night there."

"Mr. Gabrielini?"

"Yes. He was delighted to hear the news and asked me to give you a message. Do not, under any circumstances, turn your back on General Hethcutt now! He will go out of his mind, Don Giacomo says."

"I sent him a coded wire to San Francisco. I don't suppose there was any way it got to him."

"Yes, it was forwarded to Paso Robles just this morning. He says to tell you that the general could raise ten or twelve thousand in cash—more if he mortgaged his herds."

"Then we don't have to worry about a real compromise offer from Hethcutt."

They walked along together, leading Hewitt's horse. "Mr. Hewitt," Lon Tsan said, earnestly, "there is no compromise in the general, only obedience to higher rank. I have studied this man myself for years. He ruined my family's good name, and I will spend the rest of my life getting it back. It is necessary to know one's opponent, and believe me, sir, this man is a madman."

Sneaky, the puma, came bounding down the slope to meet them. He rarely came this close to the road and he was plainly surprised to see Lon Tsan back already, but as happy as he was surprised. He padded along beside them, rubbing against first one and then the other to show how happy he felt.

They left the road and cut across the wedge-shaped and barren hill that hid the Flying W from view. Bella Whiting came running to meet them. She was in a dress again, with her hair up, and wearing moccasins over bare feet.

She had a smile for both of them. Hewitt gave her a nod to say that the message had been left. Lon Tsan left them to take a shortcut to his little hut up between the house and the bluff overlooking the ocean. Hewitt and the girl walked along together, the puma bounding ahead of them.

Hewitt saw the big cat stop suddenly, crouch flat to the ground, and twist halfway around to face to their right. His mouth opened in a silent snarl. Hewitt seized the girl's arm.

"Wait a minute! He sees something."

She stopped. "Sneaky! What's the matter with you?" she cried.

The puma broke into a run up the slope, keeping a low profile with his belly to the ground but making good time. There was nothing up there that Hewitt could see except rocks, but he had never been there and he did not know what could be hidden among the rocks.

But he felt a surge of fear that came from a hunch, one of the deep kinds that he never ignored. He gave Bella a push and said, "Run for the house! Get your dad or somebody here with rifles and a shotgun. Somebody's prowling us."

"No! He'll kill Sneaky," the girl said. She broke loose and ran after the puma. "Sneaky, you come here," she cried. "Sneaky, you heard me—come here at once."

The cat charged straight up the hill, rising to his full height and bounding along as fast as a horse could run. Up there among the rocks a man stood up. A puma ordinarily would not attack a man, Hewitt knew, but this opium-smoking puma was not an ordinary one, and his opium tranquility was wearing off.

The man up there in the rocks had a Winchester rifle. He was shaking all over as he watched the big cat charge him, but he got the gun to his shoulder and fired. Plainly he missed the puma, because it kept on charging toward him, but Bella screamed and threw herself down and clutched at her left upper arm.

The man fired again, and Sneaky, caught in the middle of a leap, tumbled inertly to the ground. The man turned and ran, and then Hewitt saw another man running with him, and in no more than seconds he heard the hoofbeats of hard-running horses.

Bella was sitting up, clutching her arm and swaying

and moaning. He dropped to his knee beside her. "Grit your teeth, girl," he said. "We've got to take a look at this."

Out of the corner of his eye he saw Sneaky stagger to his feet and look around himself malevolently. There was a raw wound on the side of his head, under the left ear, not big or deep, but enough to have stunned him briefly. What it would do to him over the long term—who knew?

Hewitt took his .45 out first and laid it where he could grab it if Sneaky attacked. Lon Tsan came running and knelt too, and held Bella's arm while Hewitt used his pocketknife to cut off the sleeve of her shirt.

"A ricochet," Lon Tsan said. "I heard it hit something harder than this arm."

Part of the rifle slug lay just under the skin of the girl's arm. It had entered an inch and a half away, leaving a tiny entrance wound that could have been made by a knife blade.

"I'm all right now," Bella said. Her voice trembled, but she was over the shock if not the pain.

"What kind of medical kit do you have in the house?" Hewitt asked her.

"Some tincture of iodine and some pine-tar salve, that's all I know. Why?"

"Bella, we're going to have to open this wound up all the way, to clean it out and make sure it drains, and it's going to hurt. Can you walk to the house?"

"Oh, sure."

He helped her to her feet and put his arm around her to steady her. Behind them came Sneaky, more bewildered than angry. "Poor Sneaky!" Bella said. "Who would try to shoot him when he's here at our place and not bothering anybody?"

"I'm pretty sure they weren't after Sneaky. They were surprised by him and fired to save their own lives."

"But what were they doing there with a rifle, anyway?"

"Bella, it's a bad mess. I think they were after your dad, or me, or maybe Lon Tsan. Or maybe one of the fellows Hippo hired has a private enemy. The one thing I'm fairly sure of is that they were not lion hunting."

Alf Whiting had come out of the house with a .45 in his hand. He lost his head for a moment when he saw that his daughter had been injured. He ran to get the medical kit, and then the smooth stone on which he sharpened his razor. Hewitt sent him for his blowtorch while he honed the point of his knife to a keen edge.

"I can give you some opium to deaden the pain, Bella," said Lon Tsan.

"Oh, no—no, thanks!" She shook her head testily, although she smiled. "I don't want anything to do with that stuff."

"Sometimes it helps. If it gets too painful, say so."

"That's right," said Hewitt. "I wish you'd take a little pill of it with a glass of whiskey and water to get it started."

She consented reluctantly. Lon Tsan set off at a run up the slope to his secret grotto, while Alf Whiting brought a small shot of whiskey diluted by water. The girl chewed the tiny pellet of opium and washed it down with whiskey. Alf Whiting brought clean, white cloths with which to make a bandage.

"I've helped dress many a worse wound than that," he said, "and never turned a hair. But I can't stand to see you cut into her, Mr. Hewitt, and that's the truth."

"Then don't watch. Just fire up your torch."

Hewitt sterilized the point of his knife in the flame of the blowtorch. He waited for the knife to cool and the opium to take hold. He sliced in where the dark shadow of the bullet fragment lay just under the skin, and fished it out on the point of his knife.

It was a tiny, flat piece less than a quarter of an inch long and not quite half as wide. Bella did not wince as he brought it out. He made a shallow slash across her arm to the entrance wound. Bella grunted a little, but that was all.

"A good, clean, shallow wound," Hewitt said. "We'll wash it out with clean water from the well, and smear it with iodine and tie it up. You'll be all right in a day or two."

He dressed the arm. Bella asked him if he could dress Sneaky's wound. He shook his head. "I don't think I want to fool around with him," he said. "Look, it's not bothering him much."

The puma was already pawing at the wound, grumbling each time he gave himself pain. "I can do him more good than anyone else," Lon Tsan said. "Come with me, you rascal, and have a good smoke all by yourself."

He snapped his fingers and the puma frolicked gaily after him. Bella refused Hewitt's aid into the house. Whiting, stony-faced, went with Hewitt to talk to Hippo Thompson and the men. No, they said, there was no one who hated any of them badly enough to want to shoot them from ambush.

"Unless it's me," Hippo said. "I told Crazy Ozzie in the courthouse the other day that we still had some unfinished business."

"But would he shoot you in the back with a rifle, at long range? Wouldn't he want to shoot you down in front of an audience?"

Hippo shrugged, but Alf Whiting said, "If Lionel

Hethcutt said it would be worth ten dollars extra to get any of us out of the way, that's all it would take."

"The man's an idiot if he thinks he can get out from under this judgment by killing you, Alf," said Hewitt.

"Yes, and the general ain't that kind of idiot. I think it was you he was after."

You're probably right, Hewitt thought, but I'd like to know what makes you think that. . . . He said, "Why me?"

"You probably know more about that than I do."

Hewitt said nothing, but as he and Whiting walked back to the house, the rancher took up the subject again.

"Those Italian families have their own little world. I never was part of it, but Hethcutt is—or at least was. If I was you, Mr. Hewitt, and was fooling around with something that would set the Italians against Hethcutt, I don't think I'd turn my back on anybody."

"What makes you think I'm doing that?"

"Mr. Hewitt, I wasn't born yesterday. You was recommended to me by Lon Tsan. My little case turned out to be bigger than any of us thought it would be, but it wasn't big enough to interest your company when you came here to help. Lon Tsan's father was in the Li Fang Importing Company, and it went broke when the Taorelli syndicate went broke. There, I'm not such a fool as I look, am I?"

"Alf," said Hewitt, "I never did take you for a fool."

Whiting smiled one of his rare smiles. "I couldn't afford your company's fees, but if I can ride with my feet hanging out of the endgate part of the way, I'll do it, and I don't mind being used in somebody else's case."

By Friday, three days later, Bella's arm was still painful and she found it better to carry it in a sling, but Hewitt was pleased with the way the wound was healing. He was not so pleased at having to lie to Alf Whiting to get away with Bella to meet Mrs. Hethcutt. The girl said she wanted to buy some things in Three Oaks and that she felt safe only with Hewitt guarding her.

Whiting said nothing, but he plainly did not believe the story. The two set out together on horseback, Hewitt carrying a Henry .30–.30 carbine in a boot on the saddle. They let the horses run despite the pain in Bella's arm, and he kept his eye out as best he could in all directions.

Nearing the little crossroads town, Bella left the road and headed for a small grove in a little green and marshy glade where a windmill towered. As they neared it, Hewitt could make out a dark team and a black-top buggy. The woman in it, he saw when they reached the buggy, was white-haired. She might have been attractive at one time, but there was a grim, wild look to her now that made him think of a witch.

"Hello, Bella," she said, coldly. "What's the matter with your arm?"

"Somebody shot me," the girl replied. She dismounted and went to the buggy to kiss the cheek her aunt leaned down to offer.

"Who?" Bernardina Hethcutt snapped.

"We don't know but it was probably one of Uncle Lionel's men. He wasn't shooting at me. The pet puma that hangs around our place frightened them, and they shot at him and ran. I got nicked by a piece of a bullet."

Lionel Hethcutt's wife stared at her. "I find all this hard to believe, Bella. Lionel has been in a rage ever since that fool judge jailed him for a night—actually kept him in jail!—and then made that silly decision. All those figures—who is going to believe them?"

"I do, madam," said Hewitt.

She gave him a coldly angry look. "And who are you?"

"The name is Jefferson Hewitt. I'm full partner in a bonding and indemnity company that bonds the officers of the Tuscan-American National Bank of San Francisco. If your husband suspects that, surely he's worried about a lot worse than the judgment Alf Whiting got against him. And I think that when Bella was hit, they were shooting at me."

"The Taorelli syndicate."

"Yes, ma'am."

She looked away, sitting motionless in the buggy. "My family's name blackened, hundreds of people hurt, many ruined. Do you seriously think my husband is responsible for it?"

"I have no proof either way, but I think that you have suspected him of it for some time."

"Oh, my God!"

Bella went up and laid her hand on her aunt's arm. "Nobody wants to hurt you, Aunt Bernardina. But Uncle Bill Gabrielini can't be sentimental about such a horrible thing. Mr. Hewitt is the best detective in the world, and the Tuscan-American is paying his fees to find that missing money."

"I'd be better off dead," the older woman muttered. "Lionel is an egomaniac. Really, he's not quite ·sane. I—I'm afraid to go home. I don't think he has slept more than an hour at a time since he came back from court."

"Why don't you come stay with us?" Bella asked, impulsively. "You can share my bed."

"Child, I have no clothes except what I've got on, and I couldn't get any out of the house. I've thought of running away, but I haven't even got money for a ticket on the train."

"Don't worry about clothing," Hewitt said. "Come

home with us and we'll see that you get safely to your
family in San Francisco, if that's where you want to go."

"I couldn't face them."

"Now that you've faced up to the truth, you mean.
Madam, they've known it all along, and they're still your
family. They—"

"They called me a thief, a traitor, an outcast the last
time I was there, and I haven't had so much as a letter for
two years."

"Because," Hewitt said, patiently, "at that time you
were still defending your husband, weren't you? You refused to believe what they said about him. Believe me, it
will be different if you go up there to escape from him."

"I couldn't hide from him. He'd seek me out and—God
knows what he'd do."

"You don't have to hide from him. Move in with your
family and let them protect you. Come home with us, and
start a new life over again."

He knew he had a way with older women. He did not
raise his voice or permit himself to be drawn into argu-
ments. He simply repeated the same things over and over
in the same gentle voice, offering peace of mind, protection, and the love of family.

She broke down suddenly. The haggard shrew look
disappeared. All there was left in her now was terror to
get safely away from her husband. Hewitt tied his horse
behind the buggy and got in and took the lines of her
team. It was a good one, and he let them run, with the
.30–.30 propped up between his knees, butt down.

Bella rode first in front of them and then behind them,
patrolling the road and handling her horse with one hand.
All the time they were on the public road, Bernardina
Hethcutt was petrified with terror. Shortly after Hewitt
turned the sweating team up the squirming road to the

Flying W, she suddenly became quiet. She could believe, now.

They passed Hippo Thompson's men, building new fence, repairing old, killing time as they kept an eye out for interlopers. Alf Whiting came out of the shop where he had been repairing harness when they drove into the yard. If he felt any surprise, his face did not betray it.

"Hidy, Bernardina, it's mighty nice to see you here finally," he said.

"Bella and Mr. Hewitt said I could stay here until you could get me to San Francisco and my family. How can you let me into your house after all Lionel has done to you?" she said, beginning to weep.

"You just go right in there with Bella like it was your own home, Bernie." Alf turned to two of the new men Hippo had hired. "Get this buggy out of sight behind the barn. Put the team up in the back corral and wipe them down before you let them drink. And then one of you go bring Hippo. We're going to set up twenty-four-hour guard around this place for a while."

Sneaky came slouching into sight from his favorite hiding place under the live oaks. His wound looked ghastly, but it was healing cleanly, and Lon Tsan had kept him only semiconscious for the last few days, before departing today.

"Oh, there's your mountain lion I've heard so much about. He's beautiful, but I hope I'm not expected to let him get familiar with me" was all Hethcutt's wife said.

Chapter Nine

Hewitt did not believe for a second that Hethcutt would let his wife escape without a battle, but he let Whiting take charge of their defenses while he made arrangements to get Bernardina to San Francisco. He saddled a fresh horse and rode—hard—back into Three Oaks. It was not a scheduled stop on the Southern Pacific, but there was a depot and a telegraph operator there.

He gave the operator a wire to Gabrielini, and he could only hope that the banker would understand it:

NEED FULLEST SP HELP GET BH TO SF STOP HAVE SP REP INCOGNITO MEET ME THREE OAKS SOONEST STOP SHOW-DOWN SOON

The telegrapher was a big-bellied, sullen man with the face of a hard drinker, a man who could still do his job but who was not far from the greased skids to oblivion. The man read the wire through twice, frowning.

"This ain't signed," he said.

"The addressee will know who sent it."

"I dunno. I don't like to get into no fights between people here. I'd like to have some identification, to protect myself."

The man understood exactly what the wire said, that was clear, and he was already on edge about something. Hewitt took out a money clip and stripped off a twenty-dollar bill. Sometimes you had to go with your Sunday punch.

"Try this," he said. "See if you can get it on the wire immediately."

No answer. The telegrapher scooped up the bill and stuffed it into his pocket. He sat down at his instrument and began sending. Hewitt could send and receive a little, and he knew that here had once been an excellent wireman. But today he was in a state of nerves that made him go slow.

"You have a nice touch," he said. "Easy to read, hard to make a mistake at the other end."

"You a telegrapher?"

"An amateur, but good enough to appreciate a professional."

The sounder began chattering with train orders. The telegrapher sat down to transcribe them. Hewitt might as well have dropped dead, for all the interest the telegrapher took in him. No doubt he was dying to get drunk on Hewitt's money.

Hewitt rode to Tom Pegram's office, in his little bachelor house on the edge of town. The lawyer came to the door wearing a holstered .45. He looked relieved to see Hewitt.

"You look like a man with problems, Tom," said Hewitt.

"If I haven't got them now, I soon will have," Pegram said, closing the door. "We've just had a stab in the back. Do you know Clark Noonan?"

"I've heard Alf mention him. Keeps a store here, doesn't he?"

"Yes. He just left here. He and I have always got along, because I don't act too conspicuously friendly with him. He can still keep Hethcutt's trade. But he came here, probably at some risk, to tell me that Rex Patterson has settled his suit out of court and gone somewhere for a few weeks."

"I see. How did he find that out?"

"Rex himself stopped in and told him before he took the train north. He was in terror of his life, and happy to settle for what he could get."

"Which was around ten thousand dollars, I imagine."

"How did you find that out?"

"It's about all the cash Hethcutt could raise. Patterson still owes you your fee, Tom. He owns property here, and he has to come back sometime. Show him no mercy. A man has to stand up and be counted."

Pegram said slowly, "We practice tough law in California. We had one judge who shot another. Two or three cases, lawyers were shot after trials. Up in the mountain counties it could still happen, but I thought we were past that here."

"You're not going to let this scare you into backing out on Alf Whiting's case, are you?"

Pegram gave him a contemptuous look. "You know me better than that." He got up and went to the window. "Looks like Keener Ward is closing up for the day. He must have got hold of some money."

"Keener Ward?"

"The station agent and telegrapher."

"Damn! I just tipped him twenty dollars, and I could get an answer within a couple of hours."

"He won't be in any shape to receive it."

"Can you fix it so I can receive it myself? Get his key, or have him leave the depot open."

"I can try. We're pretty good friends. He's a drunk, but I'll miss Keener when the railroad finally gets tired of his sprees and fires him."

Pegram put on his hat and left, declining the use of Hewitt's horse. Hewitt watched from the window and saw him meet the telegrapher just as he was leaving the depot. They talked long and earnestly, and then the telegrapher hurried toward the saloon while Pegram came back to the house.

"Keener just told me something else that I find interesting. Hethcutt and four or five of his men were in town, looking for his wife. Said he was afraid her team ran off and wrecked the buggy. I hope that's not true."

"It's not, Tom, but you don't want to know any more about it."

The lawyer merely shrugged and handed Hewitt a heavy brass key.

"That's what opens the depot padlock. Keener said he was going home, but I imagine that he'll take a jug along with him. He said tell you the file copy of your wire is not in the files yet. If you need it, look under the tariff book."

"He must be scared."

"He has reason to be. There is a Bar H man still in town. I don't know him but he's riding one of Hethcutt's good horses, and it's tied in front of the saloon. From there, you can see just about anything that happens in town."

"Can you feed me something? Then I think I'll fort up in the depot and see what happens."

Pegram got out some cold brown beans and put them on to fry in an iron skillet. He made fresh coffee and put a pan of corn bread in the oven. "It's a lonesome way to live," he said, "and I surely never figured on getting into a feud when I set up practice here. But a poor man takes what he can get."

"You won't always be poor, Tom."

"If I survive, maybe. First I've got to do that, to cash in on my court cases."

Pegram was not a coward, but he was depressed and nervous and very, very alone in this town. Alf Whiting had said nothing about Hethcutt controlling Three Oaks with an iron hand. Probably he was used to ignoring Hethcutt altogether. Men like Pegram, Clark Noonan, and Keener Ward could not afford to be so independent.

They ate in silence. Hewitt stood up. "I wonder if you've got a rifle of any kind that I could borrow, just in case," he said.

"No, but I've got a double-barreled twelve, if that will do you any good."

"It might be better than a rifle."

Pegram had not only the gun, but two boxes of ammunition, all loaded with fine birdshot. Hewitt loaded the gun and stuffed his pockets full of shells. He carried the gun in plain sight under his left arm as he rode to the depot.

There was a hitching rack behind the depot, but it was too far from the building to suit Hewitt. There was a small baggage room that probably never had been used. He led the horse inside it and closed the door.

He carried the gun into the office and sat down at the bow window from which he could see both ways on the rail line. Now most of the town, such as it was, lay behind him. There was a small window in the back wall that made him nervous. He could find no cloth of any kind to cover it with, but he did find a can of black paint, the kind used to paint rail switch stands. There was no brush, but he found a rag with which he could smear the window with paint. This would force an intruder to break the glass if he wanted to peer inside.

Just before he blacked out the last of the glass, he saw

a solitary rider coming slowly from the town, a fine horse held unwillingly to a walk, the rider sitting as erect as a trooper in a crack cavalry regiment. It came to Hewitt that if Hethcutt were to make a fight over his wife's disappearance, he would think like a soldier and deploy his men accordingly.

Yonder, then, was a picket sent out to probe an enemy. Very well, Hewitt knew something about soldiering, too. The telegraph sounder was clicking away, but it was through traffic, not meant for him. He snatched up the shotgun Tom Pegram had lent him and slipped out the front door of the station. He peered around the corner, holding his hat in his hand.

Sure enough, the horse wore the Bar H brand. The rider dismounted and dropped the reins, letting the horse stand. He took out his .45 and began a slow, cautious advance toward the depot. He stopped just inside the gun's maximum effective range in the hands of a good shot, grasped it in both hands, and took a careful sight.

He was aiming, Hewitt thought, at the blacked-out window, to throw a scare into Hewitt and leave the next move up to him. Hewitt scrambled out into the open on his knees, and leveled the twelve-gauge, aiming at the man's legs. He squeezed the trigger of the half-choke barrel to give the shot a maximum-scatter pattern.

The man went down screaming, without ever getting off a shot with his .45. He could not be badly hurt, but it would take some time to pick all the fine shot out of his pelt. The horse bolted in panic, leaving the wounded man stranded.

The man stopped screaming and scrambled toward his gun, which he had dropped when the birdshot hit him. Hewitt stepped out and aimed the shotgun again.

"Just hold it right there," he called. "Move one inch toward that gun and you get the next one in your head, and it's loaded with buckshot."

The man hastily backed away from the .45 and stood up, elevating his hands. "My God, I'll be crippled for life," he said. "My legs is both shot up."

"You're all right. Where's General Hethcutt?"

"I don't know."

"You're a liar. How are you deployed? Who is your next man in rank?"

"Some fellow by the name of Buck Parrish is all I know."

"Where is he?"

"I don't know. He's supposed to check with me in Three Oaks soon."

"And you'll sure enough be there, won't you? Your horse is headed for home. Start walking back to the town, and pass the word to General Hethcutt that if it's gunfire he wants, he'll get plenty of it."

"My legs are killing me. I got a dozen wounds."

"You'll have another one that really will kill you if you don't start walking."

Yes, he was an old ex-soldier, a man who knew how far a bluff would go and when it was time to take orders. He lowered his hands, turned, and started walking back toward the town. His gait was steady, and he did not bother even to scratch the places where the birdshot stung.

Hewitt hurried back into the depot. Nothing to do now but wait, forted up in a building with his horse, where the Bar H gang could surround him and take him at their leisure. He glanced at his watch. When he heard the Three Oaks call signal, he looked at his watch again. Exactly twelve minutes had passed.

He had to cut in once and ask the operator to slow

down. AMATEUR HERE STOP TAKE IT SLOW, he sent. The brass pounder in San Francisco slowed down so Hewitt could transcribe:

> AM INSTRUCTED FULLEST AID TO J HEWITT STOP HOW DO
> I REACH HIM SOONEST QMK
>
>   ED HOYT DIV SUPT

To which Hewitt replied:

> THIS IS HEWITT STOP NEED NORTHBOUND FREIGHT STOP
> MILEPOST TWO SEVEN EIGHT BRIEFLY TAKE CLANDES-
> TINE SF PASSENGER THIS EVENING STOP DEVOUTLY HOPE
> TRAIN ON TIME STOP IS THIS POSSIBLE QMK
>
>   JEFFERSON HEWITT

The division superintendent must have been leaning over the operator, and he must have been intensely aware of pressure on him from very high places indeed. He replied immediately:

> MAY I SUGGEST ALTERNATIVE NORTHBOUND WORK TRAIN
> STOP TWO SEVEN EIGHT AT SIX-THIRTY TODAY STOP
> WILL HAVE ROW OVER ALL TRAFFIC STOP DO YOU NEED
> ARMED GUARDS QMK
>
>   ED HOYT DIV SUPT

Hewitt's answer:

> DELIGHTED YOUR SUGGESTION STOP WILL SUPPLY TWO
> ARMED GUARDS MYSELF STOP THANK YOU
>
>   JEFFERSON HEWITT

He waited only long enough to receive the acknowledgment from San Francisco. He locked the depot and led his horse out of the baggage room and locked it, too. He mounted and rode at a gallop to Tom Pegram's place, to return the agent's keys.

"How did you make out? What's up?" Pegram wanted to know.

"The less you know, the better. And don't go anywhere without that gun!" Hewitt said.

He whirled his horse and headed for the highway. Half a mile from town, he saw three riders coming toward him from the Bar H range. They spotted him about the same time that he saw them. They spurred into a hard gallop and changed direction to intercept him farther down the road.

They had to stop to open a gate a quarter of a mile ahead of him. Hewitt kept his horse pounding toward them, but suddenly he veered off the road where a wooden gate spanned a shallow ditch. He could only hope that the horse was a jumper.

He was having his luck with him today. The horse took the fence with inches to spare, without breaking stride. Hewitt was on Alf Whiting's Flying W range now, but he could take no comfort in legalities. He pulled his .45 and fired two shots into the air, and after a moment, a third one. He reloaded the gun as he rode.

He looked back and saw the three Bar H men pushing their horses hard to catch him before he reached the house. They had no chance, but neither could they go back and confess to General Hethcutt that they had not tried.

He heard two shots and then a third as Hippo Thompson and his perimeter pickets came pounding toward him. Hewitt hauled in his horse and turned it and pointed toward the men who had been pursuing him. Hippo was still concealed by the live oaks and the Bar H men were still lashing their horses hard.

Hippo, followed by four men, burst from cover with their guns in their hands. They were spotted instantly. Hethcutt's three men whirled their horses and headed for home as hard as they could go. Hewitt fired another shot to get Hippo's attention. When he had it, he motioned for Hippo to come meet him.

"I jumped the plank fence but I don't think they would try it. I think they probably left a gate open down there. Let's close it and go home," he said.

"Sure. They got their tails burned and learned a lesson," said Hippo, "and the man I want ain't in that bunch anyway."

It was years since Bernardina Hethcutt had ridden a horse, and that part of it frightened her more than anything else. She got on behind Bella, on a gentle old mare. Hewitt, Whiting, and five men made up the escort that headed down to where the rails passed through a heavy grove of oaks and crossed a dry culvert that could carry a lot of runoff water during the winter wet season.

There they dismounted at six-fifteen in the evening. Two of the men carried their bedrolls; these would ride the caboose with Mrs. Hethcutt and guard her until they reached San Francisco. Hewitt kept checking his watch.

Mrs. Hethcutt came up and took both of his hands. "I know this is just a job to you," she said, "but I want you to know that I can't say how much I appreciate your kindness—yes, and your nerve and ingenuity, too. Thank you, Mr. Hewitt. I'll feel better, once I'm back with my family."

"It's too bad it had to come to this, ma'am," Hewitt

said, "but we don't always have a choice of choices, and we have to do what needs to be done."

"This is my choice of choices. It has been unmitigated hell."

"All the same, I'm sorry, and I'm glad I could be of a little help to you."

Bella said, "Aunt Bernie, don't let it prey on your mind. I imagine Mr. Hewitt has helped break up a few marriages in the past."

She declined to meet his eyes. "As I said," Hewitt remarked, "I'm glad I could be of help. One thing is important. If you can sit down with Mr. Gabrielini as soon as possible, and tell him everything about the situation here, you could do us more good than anything else."

"I'll see him tonight," she promised.

She looked exhausted, but she had lost the haggard, shrewish look of lost hope. What hell that egotistical little martinet must have put her through! Hewitt made one more try.

"If you can think of any possible place your husband could have hidden the Taorelli syndicate loot, that's what we need."

"No one is more anxious to recover it than my own family. It's our name that has been tarnished, but I'm completely in the dark."

He gave her a reassuring smile. At six-eighteen they heard, distantly, the locomotive whistle that warned of a grade crossing. They held the skittish horses more tightly as the furious chuffing of a big engine became audible, and then the train became visible, coming from the south. A conductor in overalls was leaning out, hanging from the steps of the caboose and counting telegraph poles since the last marked milepost.

They saw each other at the same time. It was a big,

powerful engine and it had only a gang car and a caboose. It came to an easy stop and the conductor dropped
to the ground on the fly.

"Mr. Hewitt?"

"I'm Hewitt," Hewitt said, offering his hand. "You're
thirty-three seconds early."

The conductor nodded his head toward the gang car.
"The division super decided to send along a dozen
roughnecks from the extra gang. A cook, too—a good one.
The lady will be served a pretty good dinner in about an
hour, in the caboose."

"Just don't stop in Three Oaks, sir."

"We won't even stop in Paso Robles."

The foreman of the extra gang got down out of the
gang car. He had a .45 in his hip pocket and he carried a
Winchester. He gave the two guards who were waiting to
follow Mrs. Hethcutt into the caboose a skeptical scowl.

"We're really pretty good at protecting our trains and
cargoes," he said. "You might need these men worse than
I do."

Hewitt grinned and ordered the two men to bring their
bedrolls and mount up again and go home. Bella and her
aunt kissed good-bye. Mrs. Hethcutt let the conductor
boost her to the steps of the caboose. The conductor gave
the highball signal as he followed her, and the big engine
got gently but swiftly into motion.

When Hewitt and Whiting and Bella and the hands
reached the top of the hill, they could see the short train
speeding northward, making passenger-train time. With
ROW over all traffic—right of way over every other train
on the line—the division superintendent would have
earned extra marks on his record before daylight.

Back at the house, Hewitt, Whiting, and Hippo went
over plans for defense of the place. All three felt certain

that Hethcutt would try to wipe them out. An egomaniac to begin with, he had been so hard hit by losing the lawsuit that his judgment would be badly impaired. In his warped mind he would still be wearing a star on his shoulder and commanding a sector in which his irrational word was law.

"Mr. Hewitt, he won't wait, either," Hippo said, earnestly. "He'll try to burn us out, that's my guess."

Hewitt looked at Whiting. "What do you think?"

"Who in the hell ever could tell what a general would do? But I say we scatter out tonight, each man leading his horse and keeping cover. Half of us, that is. Change the guard at one o'clock. I don't see any use of forming up and riding around like fools."

When Hewitt said nothing, Whiting tilted his head and studied him. "What's on your mind, Mr. Hewitt?"

"I'm not sure. Let me think about it some more," said Hewitt. "Meanwhile let's do as you suggest. You know the lay of the land and this is familiar work to you. You take over-all command. I'll catch some sleep while Hippo is in charge until one. Then stir me out and I'll take the responsibility until morning."

Whiting picked his men and assigned them their duties with calm, methodical concentration. He warned them all to watch out for Sneaky, and not be startled into giving themselves away if the great cat got lonesome and came to someone for company. "He could be the best sentry we've got," he said. "I don't want him scared or hurt."

Hewitt had long ago trained himself to go instantly to sleep and set a mental alarm clock to awaken him whenever it was time to get up. He was sleeping in the new bunkhouse now, and with half the crew out on sentry duty and the other sleeping until time for them to go out, it was a quiet place. But he needed to think worse than he did to sleep. He lay there in the darkness for a long time, wondering if this was one of those hunches he could not afford to ignore.

He thought now that he knew where the loot from the Taorelli syndicate swindle was, and he had an idea of how to locate it. He could not go into court; he would be laughed out of court if he asked for a search warrant based merely on a hunch. It was going to take some doing.

Little by little he began to see his way . . . maybe. When there was no further profit in thinking, he simply relaxed and went to sleep with an empty mind. When he awakened, Hippo Thompson was muttering to someone just outside the door.

He lighted a lantern and stirred out the sleeping men. He let Hippo make the assignments. The big man, in his way, was like Alf Whiting—a little slow-thinking, but thorough and methodical. He might lack Alf's trained soldier's eye for terrain, but he knew this place well by now.

One by one, the men rode off to take post on their assigned positions. When the last one had gone, Hippo held Hewitt a moment for a private conference.

"Mr. Hewitt, the longer I think about it, the surer I am they'll try to burn us out. Not tonight, but in two or three days. Want to know why I figger that?"

"I do indeed."

"He thinks his wife is still here and he don't want to risk killing her. Once she's dead, there goes his last connection with the Italian families in San Francisco. But he's bound to hear that she's there in a few days."

"I think so myself, and I agree that that's when he'll go completely crazy and hit us."

"It's a pure pleasure to work with you, Mr. Hewitt. I ain't *intirely* dumb, am I?"

"Who said you were?"

"Crazy Ozzie Hyde. Yes, and lots of others, too. Because I'm so damn big, and I ain't got the handsomest face in the world, lots of people take me for some kind of a damn half-wit. All my life, I been called 'Hippo.' Ain't that a hell of a nickname?"

"I'm not so sure," said Hewitt. "I know a man in New York, a professor who studies and teaches such things. He says the hippopotamus is one of the gentlest of the wild animals, but he's got the heft to make himself respected if anyone takes liberties with him. I'll get you a copy of a book this professor wrote on hippos. It might make you wear the name with pride."

"That'd be something! I reckon you never had a nickname."

"I have to go back a long, long time, to when I was about six or seven, and just starting to school in a leaky old cabin schoolhouse in the Missouri Ozarks. I always had a cold, and we couldn't afford handkerchiefs, and I had to whip half the school before they quit calling me 'Snotty.'"

"Well, I declare! I say it again, it's a pleasure to work with you, a famous detective like you that will tell a thing like that to me."

Hewitt rode off through the darkness. He dismounted and led his horse from man to man. The sentries themselves were in constant motion, trying to watch all sides of the home ranch without half enough men for the job.

They were all edgy, nervous, and a little angry. He made sure he identified himself quickly as he approached one of them. It was a moonless night, and out here in the darkness it was easy to believe that the shadows were full of Bar H men.

Yet no one had seen or heard anything ominous. No

one complained about night duty, either. Hippo had collected a good, tough, willing bunch of men.

Something came gliding silently up to him, and it was hard not to jump and yell even after he knew it was Sneaky. He took no liberties with the cat, merely putting his hand down for the puma to smell and then scratching him behind the ears when he put his head up for it.

"Hewitt!"

He froze and jerked his horse to a stop, his hand dropping to his .45. And then he recognized the voice. It was Bella Whiting, a quarter of a mile from home, prowling for him without a man or a gun to protect her. He called her name softly.

"Bella?"

"Here. I knew Sneaky would find you. When he misses his dope he looks for his friends, and he likes you."

She emerged from the shadows and came close to him. She was wearing a shirt and old Levi's, as usual, and if he was any judge, nothing under them. She pushed Sneaky aside so she could lean against him.

"Aren't you going to kiss me?" she whispered.

"No," he said.

"Why not?"

"I've got work to do, my girl, and nothing comes between me and my work."

"A kiss wouldn't interrupt your damned work."

She would be a powerful temptation for any man. He could feel her physical magnetism through the dark, and he was aware that she was no simple girl with a simple restlessness. She thought things through, made up her own mind, and precociously went after what she wanted.

It was time to disentangle himself. "Bella," he said, "what the dickens is the matter with you? Haven't we got problems enough, without you causing your father any more problems?"

"I'm not causing him any problems. I'd be solving one for him. What's he going to do with me? He knows I'm not going to settle down on any lonesome old cow ranch. That has worried him for a long time. He remembers my mother too well, not to recognize her in me."

"And?"

"Look, I know you're the man for me, whether you do or not, because I've been looking for a certain kind of man for a long, long time, and you're him. I'm the woman for you, too, and you'd find that out soon. I would be a help, not a problem. We already *like* each other, don't we?"

"Sometimes I wonder."

"Oh, hell, now you're just being nasty. I don't believe in romantic love. I never have. If we like each other, and respect each other, and trust each other, what would be missing?"

"Bella, I just don't think I could trust you."

"You'd soon find out."

"You're talking about marriage?"

"Of course, when the time comes. When you know it's what you want and that you can trust me."

"There would be months on end when you'd never see me. I'm a man who likes to travel, and my job is nothing but travel. It's no job, no life, for a married man."

"I could travel with you sometimes, and stay close to you without bothering you. We could take some trips together, and have a home somewhere for you to come home to between jobs."

"That's a dream, an impractical dream."

"This isn't."

She put her arms around him suddenly and stood on

tiptoe, demanding his kiss. He tried to get out of it by just putting his cheek against hers, but her eager mouth sought his and he found himself kissing her back with blind hunger.

He got hold of himself, so that his voice was steady enough to say, "What did that prove? I already knew you were a very desirable woman."

She let her arms drop, but the fingertips of her right hand strayed across his cheek and stroked his mustache.

"I'm not in that big a hurry. Just try to forget it, Hewitt. Just try!" she said.

She vanished in the darkness, the big cat slinking at her heels. Hewitt caught up the reins of his horse, thinking, Damn! She really is a nice kid, and very wise. I wonder if —no, I'm not *intirely* dumb, as Hippo would say. That's not for me.

Chapter Ten

The night passed uneventfully. So did the next one, and the next one, but there was no letting down in the uneasy vigilance of the men. It took an old noncom like Alf Whiting to keep his squad keyed up this way, but Hewitt wondered what would emerge from the military mind across the line fence that separated the Flying W and the Bar H.

On the third day, Lon Tsan appeared—as usual, without warning, and as inconspicuously as possible. Hewitt wanted badly to talk to him, but he let the Chinese go up to his grotto without even exchanging greetings.

Then, one at a time, other Chinese appeared and took the same trail. Alf Whiting was out with that part of the crew that was not sleeping, patrolling the fences. Hewitt had a hunch that these Chinese did not come here to smoke opium. They looked like tough, strong waterfront workers to him.

There was no sign of Sneaky, but he was a cinch to be up there with the Chinese. Bella was busy in her kitchen, baking bread and singing as she worked. She had not once mentioned her meeting with Hewitt in the night and she seemed to be perfectly at ease with him when others were around.

When Hewitt had counted the seventh Chinese to glide swiftly and silently through the grove and out of sight, Bella came to the door. Hewitt was supposed to be asleep, but he could not sleep until he knew what was going on. Alf had slung a hammock between two trees some fifty feet from the back door, and Hewitt was resting there.

"Hewitt!" Bella called, softly.

"Yes?"

"What is this, a Chinese invasion?"

"That's what I'm wondering. I don't think it's anything to worry us, but let's let your father handle it."

She came swiftly to the hammock. He sat up, and she sat down beside him. The hammock threw them rather more closely together than he liked, but with this woman, the only safe tactic was to appear unaffected.

"I don't think Dad's going to like it," she said. "The Chinese do things their own way. They don't take orders, once their minds are made up. I wish I knew why they're here."

"So do I."

"I wonder what Aunt Bernie told them in San Francisco."

She was a sharp one. The appearance of the tough, competent-looking Chinese immediately after Mrs. Hethcutt's arrival in San Francisco could be mere coincidence, but somehow he doubted it.

Alf Whiting came walking his horse toward them. He did not seem at all disturbed to see Hewitt and his daughter sitting so snugly together in the hammock, but then his was not a face to betray emotion of any kind. He dismounted and took off his hat and wiped his face.

"Hot," he said.

"Yes," said Hewitt, "and it may get hotter. Lon Tsan is here, and so are seven other Chinese, and I'll bet you a dollar to a dime that there's not a pipe man in the bunch."

Whiting scowled. "Where are they?"

"They headed up toward the dugout, one at a time. I

have a feeling they all got off the train in Three Oaks sometime during the night, and hoofed it down here without anybody seeing them."

"They have a way of taking matters into their own hands that I don't like. I wish—"

In the grove above them, closer to the ocean bluffs, Sneaky gave a loud, long, impatient yowl. Alf's scowl deepened.

"He's not getting his smoke. He gets meaner than a rattlesnake when he's kept off it," he said.

"I like this less and less," Hewitt said. "Lon Tsan ought to know better than this. Can't you go talk to him?"

Whiting shook his head. "You have to let them do things their own way. Their family honor is at stake. In a way, it's a good sign. They must know something that we don't know, but we'll just have to wait until Lon Tsan gets around to us."

Both Hewitt and Whiting stayed near the house. The men came in for their noon meal in two shifts. Not until the second shift had gone did the Chinese appear, coming down the slope with that swift, gliding walk of his. He gave them both a courteous bow and offered his hand.

"Maybe you won't like it," Whiting said to him, "but it seems to me you're taking a hell of a free hand with my place, Lon Tsan, and you've got to quiet Sneaky down some way."

"I apologize most humbly," the Chinese said. "I brought some friends who may be a big help if the general tries to make trouble, and I had to get them out of sight quickly. I am sorry, too, about Sneaky. My friends are not addicted to the pipe, but I gave Sneaky five right under his nose, and then a couple of pills to eat in some chicken. He won't make any trouble for us."

"Lon Tsan," said Hewitt, "what the hell is going on?"

Lon Tsan shrugged. "I wish I knew. I know that Mrs. Hethcutt has left her husband, with your help, and is back with her family. I know that the Taorellis and Mr. Gabrielini have been meeting. I know that the Taorellis are able to raise sixty thousand dollars toward the bank's loss, but Mr. Gabrielini said to wait because he thought you would recover it all. That is why my friends and I are here—to help you if we can, when the time comes."

"Lon Tsan, Mr. Gabrielini is an optimist. I have a hunch or two, nothing more."

"Could you not tell me more about it?"

"Not yet. Have you ever been at Hethcutt's house?"

"Not in it, but I have been close enough to peer through his windows many times. So have some of the friends who are now with me."

"Could you lead the way for six or eight of us to take a close look at it?"

"Oh, no! That is impossible."

"How close could we get to it?"

"Ordinarily, a quarter of a mile. But if he is patrolling his place as well as Mr. Whiting is, that would be impossible now."

"Mr. Hewitt," said Whiting, "what are you planning on doing?"

"I'm not sure yet." Hewitt turned back to the Chinese. "Could you still get close enough to the house to peer into the windows?"

"I think so. He has three dogs, and they all know me now. A little meat with opium in it, and they are no trouble."

"Could you take some of your friends with you?"

"Oh, yes, at night of course."

"Could they carry big metal buckets with them?"

"It would be only a little more difficult."

Hewitt closed his eyes to think. Whiting said, "Mr. Hewitt, damn it, what are you up to?"

"Describe this place to me. Map it for me, if you can. I carry drawing paper and colored crayons. I wish you could get a detailed and accurate plat of the entire layout."

"Lon Tsan would be better at that than me," Whiting said. "I never was exactly an honored guest there."

"I will be glad to try," the Chinese said.

The bunkhouse had too much traffic in and out. Hewitt brought his little wooden case up to Whiting's house. He had always had a knack for drawing, and like his other talents, he had honed and improved it. He knew he lacked genius, but the next best thing was to be just what he was—a very good jack at many trades.

He opened the case on the kitchen table and unfolded several sheets of cheap newsprint drawing paper. With a heavy pencil he sketched the highway himself, the places where the Bar H fence was pierced by gates, and the two windmills he knew about because they were visible from the road. He handed the pencil to Lon Tsan.

"This makes it easy," said Lon Tsan. "There are only trails from the Bar H to the public road, except to Three Oaks. Here, you see, we have a wagon road, a pretty good one. It runs off the map here.

"Now we draw in the other direction. Here there is a stand of oaks, then more prairie, and here another stand of oaks about three quarters of a mile from the house. This is where the old house stands, the one used before General Hethcutt built his big yellow house on top of the hill, here."

"Wait a minute. Here's another sheet of paper. Sketch the house, describe it, and show us what else is there in larger scale."

What Lon Tsan drew was a two-story house surrounded on two sides by a roofed, Spanish-style *galeria*, a
narrow porch with an unmortared brick floor. Now Hewitt took the pencil and drew the details as Lon Tsan described them.

Here was the front door, now seldom used, but leading
to a fairly large living room. Behind the living room, and
accessible only through it, was the general's small office.
It had only high clerestory windows and Lon Tsan had
never been able to see through them. Here was the
kitchen door, here a side door that led to an arbor shaded
by heavy muscat grapevines. The vines also masked the
brick walk to the privy.

Behind all were corrals and stables and a big bunkhouse with its own kitchen and dining room. There was a
roofed, open shed in which Hethcutt kept a fine two-
seated carriage, his wife's buggy, and the green-painted
spring wagon he used now and then for light, fast trips.

Hewitt sketched these in on the first map. The house
stood in a grove of low-growing live oaks, Lon Tsan said.
There were two windmills with force pumps over deep
wells, and a storage tank that supplied the house.

"He's got a lot of money invested here," Hewitt mused.

"Yes, he has," said Lon Tsan. "The house has a heavy
stone foundation that has withstood at least two earth-
quakes. The front door is heavy black walnut with many
coats of varnish and heavy brass fittings. I have heard it
resembles the house of a big general in Washington in
many ways."

Hewitt put his finger on the grove where the old Bar H
house stood, when the ranch brand was the 88. "Is this
place used at all?"

"During haying time he sometimes sleeps men there.
There may be some there now."

"Is there any chance for us to slip in and hide there with six or eight of our men?"

Lon Tsan shook his head slowly. "There will be men sleeping there now, I am sure."

"How close could we come to it at night?"

"About here, with luck." Lon Tsan put his fingertip on the map a half mile from the old house in the grove, on the road to Three Oaks.

"And whoever is denned up there, we'd have them between us and Hethcutt's yellow house. That puts a crimp in things."

"Now, look here, Mr. Hewitt, what are you planning?" Whiting demanded, stubbornly. "I'm not a damned fool. I've done a little fighting. I don't like you or anybody else doing my planning for me."

Hewitt said, "I'm convinced of one thing, all that syndicate loot was converted into currency that would burn like wastepaper. Hethcutt doesn't know anything about jewels or investments, and if that much gold coin had been withdrawn from the banks, Mr. Gabrielini would have known about it and mentioned it to me. No, that would call too much attention to whoever was exchanging currency for gold.

"That currency is right there in the house, probably in his private office, but don't bet your rent money on that. The office would be the first place searched, if anyone ever got inside the house."

"And you figger to get inside the house?"

"Yes. If Lon Tsan and his friends can get to the house with fire buckets—metal pails filled with old rags soaked in tar and sprinkled with blasting powder—and touch off a few fires around the house to make Hethcutt think it's burning, the first thing he'll do is go straight to that money. I wish we could be mounted up in the grove there, to hit him right after the alarm goes off, while he's still in the house searching."

It was Whiting's turn to put his finger on the spot on the map where Lon Tsan had said was the closest they could approach the house. "Listen, if we're here, mounted and ready, we can either go around the grove or shoot our way through it while they're still pulling on their pants. We can be at the big house five minutes after the fire flares up."

"We'll have to come in shooting," said Hewitt. "Maybe Lon Tsan doesn't want his men exposed to gunfire."

"They are not gunmen, no," Lon Tsan said, "but they do not need to be exposed to it. They will have places to hide until it is over."

"They'll want some more buckets, too. Empty ones, so they can put out the fire if Hethcutt does what I think he'll do," Hewitt said.

"What's that?" Whiting asked.

"Throw the money in the fire if he sees he's surrounded and has to give it up anyway. Someone has got to be standing by with buckets filled from his own horse tank."

"My friends and I can do that," Lon Tsan said quietly.

"We'll form two attack parties," Whiting said. "The first will head straight for the grove and engage the crew in the old house. The second will wait until the firing there begins, and then ride around it and hit the main house. No matter how long we're held up at the old house in the grove, we'll be hitting Hethcutt at home in a matter of minutes."

"Excellent plan," said Hewitt. "Who will command what?"

"Hippo will attack the house in the grove. I'll command the other party."

"What about me? What do I do?"

"You come with me. You've got to handle Hethcutt. I reckon it sounds silly to you, but to me he's still a general and I'm still a sergeant, and them old habits are hard to break."

Bella Whiting came into the room. She still had the sling around her neck, but she did not use it often to support her arm. She crowded her way up to the table and looked at the two drawings, frowning.

"Uncle Lionel's house," she said. "In fact, his whole damn ranch."

"Bella, how often have I asked you not to swear?" her father said, sternly.

"You're going to attack them and burn them out."

"That's the last thing in the world we want to do—burn them out, that way. But we're going to attack them before they attack us again. The next time, you might not be so lucky."

"When is this going to happen?"

"Tonight, if Lon Tsan's men are up to a long hike. They've already had one today," Hewitt said.

"They're sleeping now. They'll be ready," said Lon Tsan. "They have waited long for this."

"What will I be doing?" Bella asked.

"You'll be right here," said her father. "I think maybe Lon Tsan's dugout is the place for you, with Sneaky in with you. I'll leave one man with a rifle staked out near the house here, but you stay out of sight no matter what happens!"

"You think the syndicate money is in Uncle Lionel's house, don't you?" said Bella.

"Mr. Hewitt does, and that's good enough for me." Whiting leaned over and kissed her temple. "Will you stay in the dugout with Sneaky and behave yourself? I'd like to be able to count on you."

"You can."

"Sure about that, now?"

"Dad, talking with Aunt Bernie, the way she has been mistreated, the way she hates that place, as though it was a prison where she'd been locked up, I have no pity for Uncle Lionel at all."

Lon Tsan said, earnestly, "One thing worries me, Mr. Hewitt. General Hethcutt is insane. You can't figure what a crazy man will do, and losing his wife right after losing the lawsuit has made him a lunatic. I have made a long study of his life and career. From the time he got out of West Point, he has been under great strain, trying to achieve fame and glory and become rich. I hope you take this seriously."

"I've thought of that, too," said Hewitt, "but I don't think the man's a lunatic. I think he's desperate, with his back against the wall. I think he'll be rash and may use bad judgment, but he's not unpredictable as a lunatic would be."

"I hope you're right," Lon Tsan said. "I am going to rest now. I think it would be a good idea if we all rested."

"But not in the bunkhouse," said Whiting. "We can all sleep on the grass, scattered through the oaks. I don't need much sleep. I can stay awake and stir out the men when it's time."

They went out and called the men together and told them what would be expected of them. Hippo Thompson looked a little disappointed when another, older man was chosen to remain behind to guard Bella and the place, but he brightened up when told he would command the party that would attack the old house in the grove.

The Chinese would leave in time to cross the road just at dusk, carrying their big iron smoke buckets. An hour later, all but the man detailed to guard Bella and the house would leave for Three Oaks. There they would go into the saloon and Whiting would stand treat for two drinks each, no more and no less. A man owed that to his gang now and then, and if it gave anyone the impression that Alf Whiting thought the trouble was all ended, that was fine, too.

Hewitt had one drink and then saw a lamp lighted in the little depot. He left his horse tied in front of the saloon and walked down to the station, where Keener Ward sat in the half-darkness, not quite awake and not quite asleep. He jumped when Hewitt spoke to him.

The sounder in its echo box was clicking away, but it sounded like routine traffic to Hewitt. "Sorry to disturb you, Mr. Ward," he said, "but I wondered if there had been a message for me."

"No, there ain't," Ward said.

"Then I wonder if I could ask why you're waiting here, and what you expect."

"I expect to go crazy, that's what."

Hewitt smiled. "What kind of crazy?"

"Sir, I'm a drinking man who is out of both money and credit. One drink—*one* drink!—would save my life now."

"Could you stop at one? Or at two or three?"

"What do you mean?" Ward snarled.

"If I sent a half pint down to you, could you stay here and catch any messages that come through for me before daylight?"

"Yes. You expecting one?"

"I want to send one first. There may be an answer."

"Get me a drink so I can send it."

Hewitt returned to the saloon, bought a flat half pint of fine whiskey, and rode his horse back to the depot. Ward gulped half of it down, corked the bottle, and instantly was a changed man. Hewitt's wire was to Benhart and

Company, the fictitious firm he and Conrad Meuse and
Giacomo Gabrielini used for the exchange of messages. It
would be in Gabrielini's hands within two hours:

PATIENT APPROACHING CRISIS TONIGHT STOP PLS STAY
WHERE YOU ARE STOP NO INTERFERENCE HERE AND MAY
NEED QUICK ANSWERS TO QUESTIONS

He signed it "Dr. H.," and was gratified to see the telegrapher turn to the instrument calmly, in full possession
of his faculties. Almost at once, the sounder began calling
the Three Oaks signal, with a wire for Hewitt. It came in
too fast for him to read it, but Ward caught it all without
having to ask for a repeat. Silently he handed the tran-
scribed message to Hewitt. It said:

HAVE ANALYZED EQUATIONS IN JUDGMENT IN YOUR
LETTER STOP COMPLIMENTS TO HIS HONOR ON HIS MATH
LOGIC STOP HIS RULE WILL STAND UP ON APPEAL STOP
EXCITING POSSIBILITIES FOR FUTURE STOP ARRANGE TIME
CHEYENNE SOONEST TO LEARN BOOLE YOURSELF

CONRAD

Hewitt was not surprised to learn that his partner was
an expert in Boolean algebra; in fact, he should have expected it. It would be good news to Alf, but as for Hewitt
learning it himself, one mathematician in the firm was
enough.

He returned to the saloon and showed Whiting the
wire. He had to explain what it meant, and when Whiting
had grasped it, he had to clench his jaws to prevent a display of emotion. Stony-faced, he handed the wire back.

"I wish General Hethcutt had a wire like that from
someone whose judgment he trusts," he said.

"It would be strange if he had not already received one. Maybe that's why he's feeling cornered. Either he or his lawyer—or both—would surely have gone into this by now."

Both men looked at their watches. It was hard to wait to give the Chinese time to reach the big yellow house on the hill, and find places to set off their firepots. At eleven o'clock they mounted up and let Hippo and his men take the lead.

Whiting, Hewitt, and five men waited ten more minutes and then followed slowly and as silently as possible. To Hewitt, the fact that there were no Bar H men in town was encouraging. Whatever plans the general was making, he wanted his crew close at hand.

Chapter Eleven

It was as dark a night as Hewitt could remember. There was no moon, and a cloud cover shut off the pallid light of the stars. Whiting pulled them up, and they left the road when he thought he was within a quarter mile of the old house in the grove.

They could hear, distantly, the barking of a dog, and then another. Plainly it worried Whiting, but Hewitt thought he knew what it meant. The Chinese had reached the big yellow house, but it would be strange indeed if they were not prepared to silence the dogs with a dose of opium in a piece of meat. How else had they gotten close enough to peer through the very windows before?

Sure enough, the dogs stopped barking. "I think we could move up a little, Alf," Hewitt said, in a low voice. "Better be prepared, though, for a one-man ambush here and there, once we break for the house. He's not likely to leave himself unprotected that way. We didn't."

Whiting gave the soft order and led the way at a walk. A blacker black appeared ahead of them—the grove surrounding the old house, where Hippo and his men should be in hiding now. Whiting started to circle it to the left.

Suddenly a gunshot rang out far ahead of them. A man shouted, and then another, and another.

And then suddenly there was a huge bloom of yellow light, high up on the hilltop above them. Whiting put his horse into a run. Hewitt followed, with the men strung out behind him.

Just as suddenly there was a rattle of gunfire behind them, in the grove at the old ranch house. Someone was pumping .30–.30 bullets as fast as he could work the lever and pull the trigger—and Hippo Thompson had carried a Henry carbine.

A man screamed, the kind of scream a man let out when he was hit. Then there was silence for a few minutes before they heard horsemen thundering straight up the road.

Hippo had knocked out the defenses in the grove and was charging the big house itself. Whiting dug in his spurs. His horse broke into a hard gallop, Hewitt and the crew following. More gunfire broke out up at the house. They hit the steep slope of the road and saw the entire house outlined behind a wall of bright, orange flame.

"No more shooting, you goddamn fools!" came Hethcutt's quivering shout of rage. "Somebody cover me. I've got to go inside. You're shooting each other, you crazy sons of bitches."

Men were running wildly in all directions. Someone was shouting, "Get buckets, get buckets! Start a bucket brigade." Whiting drew his .45 and fired once in the air, to notify Hippo where he was. Hippo's answer, another single shot, came from no more than two hundred yards to their right.

The two groups of attackers merged and charged straight up the hill. A man was dropping the bars of a corral, to lead out a saddled horse, vividly outlined in the light from the fire. Hippo stood up in the stirrups and shot twice with his carbine.

The man went down. The terrified horses streamed out of the corral, jumping the bottom rail and taking the sad-

dled horse with them. Another man loomed up in the
light to their left. Hewitt saw him first.

He reached under his coat and twisted the .45 in its
trick holster as he drew it. He snapped two shots from too
far away, but he had his luck with him tonight. The man's
leg buckled and he went down, yelling, and kept yelling
as he rolled toward the darkness.

"Split around the house!" Whiting yelled. "Drop anybody that ain't Chinese that gets in your way."

Hewitt followed him around the back of the house. A
short, muscular Chinese ran out, waving his arms. Hewitt
hauled his horse back on his haunches. The Chinese
pointed, and around the corner came General Hethcutt,
shouting at the top of his voice:

"Give me a hand, somebody. Where the hell is everybody? Give me a hand, goddamn it!"

Hewitt tumbled out of the saddle and handed the reins
to the Chinese. "Hide him back in the dark somewhere,"
he said.

Hethcutt was already plunging through the smoke into
the kitchen door. Hewitt ran after him. "Where are you?
What do you want?" he called.

"I need help. Are you deaf as well as dumb?" came
Hethcutt's furious voice.

The kitchen was full of smoke. Hewitt plunged through
it behind the general, both men coughing and choking.
On through the kitchen they went, and into the big pan-
try. It too was full of smoke, but flames from the window
gave them some light.

The general was in pants and undershirt, his long hair
disheveled. He began tearing at a pile of stacked boxes of
canned goods, dumping box after box on the floor. Plainly,
between the dense smoke and his own hysterical excitement, he did not recognize Hewitt, and probably thought

him one of the riffraff strangers he had been hiring lately.

"Stand there like a dummy, why don't you help?" he snarled. "I've got to get that one."

He did not look up as he pounded one wooden carton marked *Yellow Cling Peaches in Heavy Syrup.* Hewitt began throwing cartons, too. Hethcutt tore at the peach carton, trying to pull it out of the pile. A stack of boxes came tumbling down on him, knocking him flat.

Hewitt covered him as well as he could with his body. "Here, sir, give me a hand and we've got it," he said.

The smoke was heaviest down near the floor. The general was coughing and choking like a dying man, but he caught his end of the peach carton and let Hewitt take the other. It was far too light to contain canned peaches, that was sure.

"This way, through the front door," the general gasped. "Not such a heavy fire there." He suddenly burst into tears. "Dirty sons of bitches, they set fire to my house. Now I'll never get my wife to come back here."

There was a formal dining room, smoke-filled, and then they were in a big parlor where the smoke was not so heavy. Hewitt let go of the carton and jerked out his .45. The general shouted a curse as he felt the carton dropped.

He whirled, with eyes that streamed tears from the smoke. Hewitt had to jam the muzzle of the .45 into his stomach.

"This is as far as we go, Hethcutt," he said. "Calm down, it's not a fire. Nothing's going to burn."

Hethcutt rubbed his eyes with the sleeve of his undershirt on his left hand, and tried to get the carton under his right arm. He was not even aware of the gun in Hewitt's hand, and too blinded by smoke to see that the fire was already dying out in the buckets set under the windows around the *galeria*. He swung a fist at Hewitt, weeping with rage.

"You son of a bitch, if you're not going to make yourself useful, get out of my way," he gasped hoarsely.

Hewitt reached out and bunched the man's undershirt in his hand and jerked him close. "You damned fool, don't you recognize me? It's Hewitt," he said. "There's no fire. I'll take possession of this."

He put his foot on the peach carton that did not hold peaches. Hethcutt still did not realize the truth. He came blindly at Hewitt, fists pumping hard. He was smaller than Hewitt, and much older, but so hysterical with rage and fear that he could not be handled mercifully.

Hewitt backed away, holstering the .45. Hethcutt, weeping with rage, again wiped the tears away with the sleeve of his undershirt. He stooped to pick up the peach carton.

Hewitt reached into his hip pocket and came out with his favorite weapon, the shot-filled sap. With his left hand he caught the general by the belt and yanked him backward. He tapped him lightly on the back of the head with the sap, using a snap of his wrist rather than a swing of his arm.

The general collapsed inertly. Outside, the firing had stopped, and Whiting was rapping out orders like the old sergeant he was.

"Build a fire over there under those trees and get their wounded there. Disarm everybody. I'll hold you all responsible if anybody gets away." He raised his voice. "Hewitt! Where the hell are you?"

"In here, Alf, in the living room," Hewitt replied, calmly. "I've got the general limp as a cold snake, and I've got what we came for, too."

The Chinese had already drenched the fires in the

smoke buckets. Hewitt picked up the carton under one arm and caught Hethcutt by the wrist and dragged him toward the front door. He had to let go of Hethcutt to unbar the door, but then he dragged him out into almost total darkness.

"Give me a light, somebody. It's Hewitt, and I've got what we came for," he called.

Hippo Thompson got to him first. He offered to take the carton, but Hewitt shook his head, and Hippo threw the general over his shoulder and carried him over to where Whiting had mustered his prisoners around the fire he had built.

"Just dump him there and plant your foot on his chest if he tries to move, Hippo," Hewitt said. "Alf, keep track of this box. Nobody opens it, nobody lays a hand on it. Did we get everybody?"

Whiting took a swift count. "We didn't have a man hit, but we wounded four of theirs and have thirteen prisoners."

"Where's Crazy Ozzie?"

"I saw him, but—" Whiting took a quick look around and cursed bitterly. "We had better get the hell home. I don't like this. That ape could still kill some of us."

Hethcutt was still unconscious and, Hewitt knew, might be for another hour. They hitched one of Hethcutt's teams to a wagon and put the unconscious man in it. Hewitt carried him in his arms. He looked tiny, unkempt, and suddenly ancient, fleshless, and weak.

Hethcutt was moaning and trying to sit up soon after they passed through Three Oaks. Hippo, standing up in the wagon box to drive the team, put them to a gallop when they reached the highway. The painful jolting brought the general to full consciousness. He clutched at the edge of the wagon box and looked around.

The first thing he saw was Hewitt, riding along beside the wagon. "What the hell is going on?" he asked, vacantly. Before Hewitt could answer, he saw the peach carton in the rear end of the wagon. To Hewitt he looked like a man whose world had come to an end. He lay down on his side, resting his face on his crooked arm, and ignored the world.

At the ranch, the Chinese hurried up to the dugout to tell Bella that her father wanted her to stay there until daylight. Five minutes later, just as they brought the peach carton into the kitchen, Bella came in, slamming the screen door in Sneaky's face. Hewitt held his temper with difficulty, but now the brat was here, she might as well make herself useful.

General Hethcutt sat in a kitchen chair, with Hippo Thompson standing guard over him. Little by little, his mind was beginning to work again. A wave of the red of fury swept across his face as Hewitt brought the peach carton to the kitchen table and put it in the center.

"I think we're going to have to organize teams to get a count on this in a hurry," Hewitt said. "Bella, get some paper and pencils, and then you work on that side of the table, away from the door."

Suddenly the general spoke in a cracked voice that threatened to break into a falsetto. "I warn you," he said, "that if you open that box, I'll not rest until every son of a bitch of you is either dead or in the penitentiary."

Hewitt took out a cigar and lighted it. "I'm afraid that's a chance we're going to have to take, Hethcutt," he said.

Hethcutt shook a trembling finger at him. "I order you to put that box down here at my feet. At once! I order you to do so."

"I'm afraid you're outranked here, my friend," Hewitt said. "The sergeant's in command now."

Whiting was plainly uncomfortable, and Hewitt was fairly sure it was not mere rank that made him so. He was afraid Hethcutt would talk, that was it.

Someone brought a claw hammer and a pry bar. Hewitt drove the bar under the wooden top of the box and levered it off, board by board. Under it was a layer of heavy, waxed paper. He opened the paper carefully and there it was, stack after stack of packages of currency. He glanced from it to Hethcutt.

"Would you care to save us the trouble of counting and tell us how much is here?" he asked. And when the general merely glared, he went on, "How are you going to account for this? You carry a hell of a lot of pocket money, it seems to me."

He began stacking the packets of money for the counters—himself, Whiting, Bella, Lon Tsan, and another of the Chinese. The work went swiftly. Most of the money was in one-hundred-dollar bills, but with several packets of fifties.

It was daylight before they had counted the hoard and then double-counted it, exchanging stacks and counting one another's stack. The total came to $452,500. Hewitt sent a pair of armed riders on good horses to Three Oaks, to dispatch two telegrams. He gave them money to buy Keener Ward another half pint of whiskey, if he needed it to get in shape to send.

The first wire went to Benhart and Company, San Francisco, which meant it would be in Giacomo Gabrielini's hands twenty minutes after it was received in the telegraph office. It merely said:

EXCESSIVE RECOVERY IN HAND STOP COME HELP COUNT STOP DECISIONS NEEDED URGENTEST

To Conrad Meuse, he said:

PACKAGE RECEIVED AND TOO BIG STOP NOTIFY GIACOMO
ASK IF WE CAN RESTORE UNCLES SHARE

He let Whiting read the wires before the two men sped off to dispatch them. Clearly, Whiting did not like what was happening, but it took him a few minutes to decide what to do. He asked Hewitt to go out and sit on the woodpile with him.

"Get some rest, have a cup of good, strong coffee, and talk a few things over," he said.

"I think it's time for that myself," said Hewitt.

They sat on the woodpile a long time, sipping coffee that to Hewitt had never tasted better in his life, before Whiting could nerve himself to speak.

"I reckon you know, Mr. Hewitt, that that money don't all come from the Taorelli syndicate swindle," he said. "I reckon when you said 'uncle' in that telegram you meant Uncle Sam. If you did, he's not going to get back a cent."

"I'm quite sure of that. There's still too much of it. Unfortunately, I don't know what it will take to meet the creditors' claims in that case, but I do know that my firm is going to take a percentage of everything for our fee."

"Oh, sure, you're entitled to that. I can tell you exactly how much they got away with in the syndicate swindle."

"How much?"

"Two hundred and sixty-five thousand."

Hewitt had to make an effort to keep his face from showing his jubilation. If he and Conrad took just 10 per cent of the syndicate recovery, that fee would come to $26,500. It was not the largest fee that Bankers Bonding and Indemnity Company had ever earned, but it was one of the largest.

"That leaves," he said, "one hundred and eighty-seven thousand, five hundred dollars still to be accounted for. I'll assume that part of that money—say, fifty-four thousand, one hundred and fifty-eight dollars and seventy-three cents, which the court awarded you in real damages—was earned by the operations of the Bar H. If you also collect punitive damages to bring the amount up to seventy-five thousand, we still have one hundred and twelve thousand, five hundred dollars to account for."

Whiting buried his face in his hands. "Mr. Hewitt," he said, between his rigid fingers, "there just ain't no way you can trace that money, and if you could, I'm a ruined man. And part of it was a wedding gift to them from the Taorellis—twenty thousand. And I know that the general inherited forty thousand or so from a relative ten or twelve years ago."

"Very well, then, let's see what we have," Hewitt said. "The better prepared we are to talk figures with Giacomo, the happier I'll be."

He wrote on a piece of paper:

Taorelli syndicate swindle	$265,000
Court judgment to Whiting	75,000
Bernardina's dowry	20,000
General's inheritance	40,000
Total	$400,000
Amount recovered	452,500
Unaccounted for	$ 52,500

Whiting merely glanced at the paper, as though these figures had long been burned into his mind. Hewitt finished his coffee and cigar and let him think it over. He saw Bella come to the door with the coffeepot and look at

them questioningly. He nodded, and she brought the pot
out, filled their cups, and went back into the house without speaking.

Smart girl! She knew her daddy was in big trouble, and
probably had known it for a long time. There would have
been just too much talk in the family, when the syndicate
went broke, for her not to have heard enough to have at
least a good idea of how Alf Whiting had financed the
Flying W.

He laid his hand on Whiting's shoulder. "Let's take the
hair off, Alf, and look at some bare skin. Did you get the
general into it, or did he get you into it?"

"That little son of a bitch never had the brains or the
nerve to do anything himself," Whiting said. "He just cut
himself into the deal afterward and walked off with a
commanding officer's share when he retired. Everybody
was grabbing with both hands when the Army reduced
forces after the Indian wars. I was the only one ready with
a plan."

It came pouring out of him, a mass of detail that
showed him to be a man of remarkable memory. Giacomo
Gabrielini had penetrated to the guts of the case, but even
he had had no idea how big it was—or how well organized.

A man like Hethcutt, a staff officer most of his life but
with some experience in field command, would be in an
ideal position to crack the case before it got started, had
he so desired. Instead, his own avarice had been aroused,
and he had taken a sort of invisible command of the entire looting project. He and Whiting had met only once,
when Hethcutt got himself ordered to tour the western
posts and set up survey parties to value the surplus property.

When a thing became worthless, the Army "surveyed it

off," after a survey board had made an inspection and signed a report. Anything recovered from the sale of junk was returned to Army funds as "salvage." As a company clerk at the Presidio of San Francisco, years and years ago, Hewitt himself had clerked for many a survey board that was attesting property as useless and selling it for salvage.

It was a good system—when it worked. Whiting thought he had everything covered when brevet General Hethcutt came, with his retinue, to the post. When three days passed without the general sending for him and his captain to explain a few things, he was sure he had covered his tracks. The captain commanding the post would have been as bewildered as any outsider, Whiting said.

Whiting had moved into a vacant house that had been part of married officers' quarters, and was doing his own cooking and keeping his coded records in a footlocker under a trap door in the floor. He was whittling a little wooden dog for the son of one of his men by lamplight one evening when there came a knock at the door. He did not bother to get up.

"Come in. It's not locked," he called.

The door opened. Whiting shot to his feet when he recognized Hethcutt. Hethcutt closed the door carefully behind him and made sure it was locked.

"Sit down, Sergeant Whiting," he said. "This is informal and confidential. I will do most of the talking. I hope it will be friendly talk, but it will be necessary for you to keep in mind at all times the difference in our rank. I said, *sit down!*"

Whiting sat down, seeing the handwriting on the wall behind the taut, spare, erect figure of the officer. Hethcutt pulled up a chair near the table and sat down, too. He leaned across the table, bringing his head close to Whiting's, and with his hand took the knife and the piece of half-carved wood out of Whiting's hand and laid it aside.

"You can come back to that later," he said. "First, I want you to count out fifty thousand dollars. I'll return to my quarters while you do it, and bring back a small canvas valise that I have for the money. By then you will have convinced yourself that it would be far wiser to take a sergeant's share and let it go at that. Happily, Sergeant, quite happily!"

Whiting had hated Hethcutt ever since then. The pressure to steal more and more and more became immense, and Hethcutt could bring in enough senior officers to make it possible. But only Whiting ever saw the general himself take money.

It was clear to Hewitt that the general had had something else he could have used as a threat to Whiting, but there was no use going into that now. All he could do was reassure Alf that the statute of limitations had run out, even if papers enough to run an audit could be found after all these years.

"One more question, Alf," he said. "Where the dickens did Hethcutt get hold of Crazy Ozzie Hyde?"

"Stole him from me." Whiting's voice was cold and grim. "Minute he started dickering for the old Eighty-Eight property, I knew he meant to have mine, too. I knew Ozzie in Arizona. He was crazy as a pet coon, but oh how he could handle a six-gun! I paid him fifty a month, more than I could afford. And still he quit me to work for the general—I hear for a hundred a month."

"Then that's what he'll be fighting for, that one-hundred-dollar job. He hasn't left the country, we can be sure of that. Among all the details still undone, I'd say he rates number one. Even so, there are several things we've got to do, and do quickly."

They returned to the house, where the money had been repacked in the peach carton, which still stood on the table. In a corner of the kitchen, Hethcutt sat on a straight-backed chair, with Hippo Thompson keeping guard over him. In another chair sat Lon Tsan. His eyes never left Hethcutt.

The general appeared to have recovered some of his poise. He had to have the thick-skinned ego of the biggest grizzly bear in the Rockies, Hewitt thought. He had straightened out his flowing hair and smoothed his mustache, and he held his hat on his lap with hands that did not tremble.

"Mr. Lionel Hethcutt, I am a field agent for Bankers Bonding and Indemnity Company, the bonding agent for Tuscan-American National Bank of San Francisco," Hewitt said. "I herewith place you under citizen's arrest for defrauding that bank. You will be held in custody here until the legally constituted peace officers of the county can take charge of you. I warn you that anything you may say may be used against you in court, and that whatever means necessary will be employed to keep you in custody."

Bella Whiting came into the room from the bedroom. She had changed to a simple dress of pink-checked gingham, and had arranged her hair in a graceful mass on top of her head. She looked older, sure of herself, and very, very pretty.

The general struggled to control himself for a minute. It was a losing battle. He shouted out a single obscenity, two words, at Hewitt.

Around came Hippo's heavy hand, striking Hethcutt across the mouth in a backhand slap and knocking him from the chair. Hippo reached down and caught the general's shoulder with one hand and easily slammed him back into the chair.

"Mind your tongue around ladies," he said. "Talk all you want, but watch your language."

Hethcutt's mouth was bleeding but he did not deign to notice it. He folded his arms and sat staring stonily at the carton of money.

Hewitt drafted a telegram to Sheriff Macklin Hale in San Luis Obispo, and asked Whiting to get another pair of riders out to take it to Three Oaks. In it he said:

HAVE MADE CITIZENS ARREST OF LIONEL HETHCUTT FOR FELONY EMBEZZLEMENT OF SOME FOUR HUNDRED THOU-SAND DOLLARS STOP MONEY RECOVERED AND IN CUSTODY WITH HETHCUTT STOP URGE YOU TO TAKE EARLIEST AC-TION TO RECEIVE PRISONER AND MONEY GIVING RECEIPTS FOR SAME

FIELD AGENT JEFFERSON HEWITT
BANKERS BONDING AND INDEMNITY CO

"It won't do any good," Whiting said, when he read it. "You mark my words, Hale will be sick in bed when he gets this."

"I imagine Giacomo Gabrielini will get here first any-way, with the appropriate San Francisco authorities," Hewitt said. "We're going to have to post twenty-four-hour guards until somebody takes both the prisoner and the money off our hands, and we've nailed Crazy Ozzie."

"Now you're talking," Hippo said, softly.

Chapter Twelve

The afternoon wore on. With Whiting in command, Hewitt felt he could treat himself to a long nap. He did not undress, but merely removed his boots and lay down on a bunk in the bunkhouse. Immediately he was asleep.

It was almost dark when he awakened. He stepped into his boots, washed in cold water at the basin just outside the bunkhouse door, and walked to the house. A single lamp, turned low, illuminated one window. One of Whiting's men appeared out of the shadows, hand on his .45. He recognized Hewitt and apologized.

"Nothing to apologize for," Hewitt said, pleasantly. "Where's the sergeant?"

"In the house. He says this is his command post."

"Where's the prisoner?"

"He wouldn't give his word not to try to escape, so Alf chained him to the bedstead. Maybe he can get away," the man said, with a twisted grin, "but he'll be dragging eight feet of chain and an iron bedstead behind him."

"Where's the girl?"

"Not here. I understand she's with the Chinese. Go on in. Alf's waiting for you."

Whiting looked tired, and was showing his age. It was not regret that sapped his strength. Given the same chance again, he would have cleaned out the War Department in the same fashion, to beat the officers to it.

But obviously Hethcutt was still pulling rank on him,

and a man with Whiting's long career as an enlisted non-com had filled him with an ineradicable awe of a general officer, even one of brevet rank. And he still distrusted the civilian law of the statute of limitations. The Army would get to him some way, he would be thinking. It always did.

"No sign of Crazy Ozzie?" Hewitt asked him.

"No. Crazy Ozzie always takes care of Crazy Ozzie first. I wonder if we didn't misjudge him. I wonder if he didn't just light a shuck out of the country the minute the firing began."

"Bet on it, he didn't. Hethcutt would see to it that he always owed Crazy Ozzie money. I'll bet he's right on the place here, right now."

Something was making a noise at the screen door of the kitchen. Swearing under his breath, Hewitt ran back to let Sneaky into the house. The big, sleek puma's wound was healing, and probably was extremely tender, but Lon Tsan had filled him with the joy smoke and he was thoroughly satisfied with the world except that he wanted something to eat.

Hewitt found a big kettle filled with a cold beef roast. He began slicing off chunks and tossing them to the cat, which caught them in midair and purred like a pussycat as he gulped them down. He ate an enormous meal—you could feed two or three heavyweight fighters more cheaply, Hewitt thought—and did not object when Hewitt put the kettle away. Sneaky returned to the door, which Hewitt had closed.

"Alf!" Hewitt called. "Come here."

Whiting appeared in the kitchen doorway. "Did you feed him? Then you can let him out. He'll go back to the grotto and sleep it off now."

"That's just what I'm afraid of. He can lead Crazy

Ozzie straight to your daughter, man! Has he ever walked on a leash?"

"Why, Bella used to lead him around on just a length of chalk line when he was feeling good, but that was several years ago."

"Have you still got the chalk line? It's worth trying."

Whiting got the ball of strong, hard twist-cotton cord out of the cabinet. The big cat did not seem to know or care when Hewitt carefully tied a chokeproof bowline around his neck. When Hewitt opened the door, the cat had to be nudged outside, but then he started with his low, graceful, gliding walk up the slope.

Hewitt paid out the cord until the puma was on a twenty-foot leash. He began following, the line wrapped around his left hand, his right hand on his .45. He had trouble controlling his breath. Every nerve was on edge. He knew, he *knew*, that Crazy Ozzie was not far from here. He did not know how he knew it, but he had learned long ago never to disregard one of these hunches.

He froze, hearing the light footsteps of a woman in moccasins coming down the slope. Sneaky struggled against the cord, growling deep in his throat. Hewitt let him yank him a step or two and then could stand no more. He hauled back on the line and stopped the puma, at least for a moment.

"Go back, Bella, go back!" he shouted. "Get under cover and be quick about it."

"Sneaky got out," came the girl's voice. "I've got to find him or—"

He cut in furiously, "I'm bringing him. For God's sake, get back to Lon Tsan. Don't you ever *think?*"

He was too late. He heard the crash of heavy footsteps, and a smothered scream from Bella. He let go of the cord and ran blindly through the trees, trying to find where the sound came from.

Suddenly, there they were. It was too dark to recognize anybody, but some man had Bella down on the ground, unconscious, and was trying to throw her over his shoulder.

All Sneaky wanted to do was join the fun, but his leap hit the man in the back and knocked him down, with Bella under both the man and the cat. The man rolled over on his back.

"Ha, you thought I's fool enough to be took from behind," Hewitt heard him say.

He must have seen the horribly wounded face of the puma within inches of his nose. He let out a bawl of horror. A .45 blazed twice. Sneaky's scream showed that he had been hit.

Everything that moved would be his enemy now. Hewitt ran toward him through the dark, gun raised. He thought the puma's hindquarters were paralyzed, but he had the man down on his face and was getting his grip on the back of his neck. And Bella was still under both of them.

Hewitt shouted at the cat and ran in until his knee was against the puma's ribs. Sneaky turned and reached for him, dragging his hind legs. Hewitt waited until the big head with its bared fangs was no more than a foot away. He pulled the trigger.

Sneaky dropped. Hewitt was sure he had shot him through the brain, but he found the animal's head on the ground with his left hand, and pumped another .45 slug into it to be sure.

The man was either unconscious or paralyzed by terror. Hewitt turned him over, and even in the dark he could see that he had been too late. Sneaky had broken the man's neck with one twisting bite of his powerful jaws.

One other thing was clear. It was not Crazy Ozzie.

Bella was moaning softly. The Chinese came running as silently as possible down the slope. As he reloaded the two chambers in his gun, Hewitt called to them, "Go back, Lon Tsan—go back where you were. There's another one around here somewhere."

Men were running up from the house, too. He stood up and shouted, "Go back, go back! Everybody stay out of my way. That silly little Crazy Ozzie is hiding out here somewhere, and I don't want to hit one of you when I have to take his pants down and fan his britches."

Silence, except when Bella squirmed. He put his hand on her shoulder and pressed her down. Again he raised his voice angrily:

"If you get in my way again, Bella, I'm going to paddle you the same as I will that little piss-ant of a Crazy Ozzie. He's out there hiding in the dark somewhere, scared stiff, and when I smoke him out, I want to be sure it's him."

He patted her cheek to make her—he hoped!—understand. He stood up, felt his way around the dead man and the dead puma, and walked to the nearest tree. He pressed against it, letting it protect his back.

"You cowardly little snipe, all your life you've been running, and you're still running when you're a full-grown man. It's just us now, and it's not so much fun, is it? That's the hell of it with being a yellow son of a bitch of a coward."

"Pull your gun when you see me, because that's what I aim to do," a trembling voice screeched. "Nobody talks that way about me. Nobody calls me that name."

He came blundering through the dark, his head visible

above the skyline from thirty feet away. "I see you, Crazy Ozzie," Hewitt called. "Just keep coming and you're a dead man."

He knew there were few men in the world who were his equal at the maximum range of a .45, and he did not intend to let this depraved little gunnie come too close. He saw a shape blundering down the slope toward him. He stepped away from the tree and called, "Now, Ozzie, go for your gun as soon as you can see me."

He twisted the .45 out of its holster and took his time. He let Ozzie get off the first shot, knowing it would go high because these mad badmen tilted their guns up from the hip at point-blank range to make their kills. He drew his bead carefully and fired at the orange cone of flame that blazed out of the muzzle of Ozzie's gun.

He heard no sound except the toppling of Ozzie Hyde into the grass that grew so thinly between the trees. "Stay here," he whispered to Bella, and began walking carefully toward where either Ozzie, dead or alive, would be.

Suddenly Hewitt saw him, slumped forward in a sitting position. As he took another cautious step forward, Crazy Ozzie Hyde fell over inertly. Hewitt knelt beside him and struck a match.

"Get some lanterns up here, Alf," he called, "and get Bella back to the house. It's all over."

———◆———

"What I don't understand," said Giacomo Gabrielini, "is how you were so sure the booty would all be in currency. It still bewilders me, that the general would be such an idiot."

"I'm not sure I ought to tell you," Hewitt said. "We have our trade secrets, too. I'm sure you keep a few secrets in the bank's operations."

"But, by heaven, this is probably crucial to those very

operations," Gabrielini pleaded. "What happened once could happen again, unless I know how to prevent it."

"I would not press too hard," said Conrad Meuse. "Sometimes, my friend, it is better not to know too much."

Three months had passed. The three of them, and Nick Taorelli, the young cousin who now spoke for Bella and Bernardina's family, were sitting at a table in a private room at Gabrielini's favorite San Francisco restaurant. They had returned only today from San Luis Obispo, where the judge had signed the sheaf of papers that authorized the division of the currency found in the big yellow house. The banker had a three-foot napkin tucked into his collar and the armholes of his vest, and was skillfully eating spaghetti in a clam sauce. Hewitt envied him his mastery of the pasta.

Gabrielini put his fork down to drain a big glass of wine. He had already drained several, but he showed none of the effects.

"I am a determined man, friend Hewitt," he said, "as well as an important client of your firm. I will not be put off. You have made a big fee in this case, and I have a right to know what I paid for."

"I defer to my partner's judgment," said Hewitt.

Both Italians looked at Conrad Meuse, who had a real talent for eating spaghetti, too. He could even make it look dainty.

"Why me?" he asked Hewitt.

"Background is your part of the job and we're talking about background now. Go ahead, break their hearts," said Hewitt.

Conrad adjusted his pince-nez and pearl tiepin, which was marvelously brilliant under his neatly trimmed beard. He was dressed in his best, and had been relieved when

Hewitt turned up in a frock coat, ruffled white shirt, and stock. His only criticism had been that Hewitt would not use a touch of eau de cologne, which he regarded as a gentlemanly necessity.

"So!" he said to Gabrielini. "You wish to know what you have paid for."

"I do," said the banker. "Why won't you be frank with me?"

"Because you did not pay for it."

"*What?*" both Italians said at the same time.

"Exactly." In moments of stress, Conrad's speech had a distinct German accent, and it came out almost "eggzacdly."

"Damned if I understand," said Nick Taorelli.

"Then listen. While Jeff was performing his duties here, I was digging up certain facts that were available to me. General Hethcutt, I am sure, had devoted his entire twenty-six years in the Army, plus the time he spent in the mercantile business, to stealing everything he could safely lay hands on, and he is surely one of the cleverest as well as one of the biggest thieves in the War Department's history."

"I'll be damned!" said Gabrielini.

"An understatement, if you will permit me to finish my little recital. Through sources of my own, I was able to locate four bank accounts he maintained, in Baltimore, New York, Albany, and St. Louis. The total in them, with accrued interest, was something over a quarter of a million dollars, and the early deposits went back more than twenty-five years."

"I thought all such information was confidential," said Gabrielini, sternly. "If you ever ask me for that kind of information, I shall refuse you."

"If you do," said Conrad, "and I have good reason to

feel that it is evidence of a felony, I shall cancel your bond."

"Blackmail!"

"No, merely my duty to help preserve the sanctity of our banking system."

The banker had to fortify himself with another glass of wine. "Let us table that debate for a moment," he said, "and get back to General Hethcutt."

"Quite! The crimes which gained the general that quarter of a million dollars are no longer actionable under the statute of limitations. The same, of course, is true of the peculations he and Mr. Whiting engaged in before both men retired."

"In short," said Hewitt, "it was Hethcutt's money, and the Army could whistle for it."

"But I made a deal," Conrad went on, "with the War Department. If Jefferson could persuade Hethcutt to sign over those four accounts to the government, the said government would not intervene in our case out here. It is every citizen's duty to help his government recover stolen money, and even the thief's earned interest on it."

"Especially," said Nick Taorelli, "when you can protect a handsome fee for yourself."

"Yes, that sometimes happens, but I assure you that the public interest comes first," Conrad said, piously.

"Of course, of course!" said Gabrielini. "I imagine that friend Hewitt was motivated by the public good when he insisted that Lionel Hethcutt be allowed to retain seventy-five thousand dollars of the money found in his house."

"That's right," said Hewitt. "The War Department couldn't have laid hands on that money because the statute of limitations had already run out on the crimes that produced it. But if they had intervened in the case by filing a suit in federal court, every cent in that peach carton would have been impounded for years. In the end, the lawyers would have got it all. Hethcutt understood that and was quite willing to deal."

"What deal?" Gabrielini demanded.

"Well, I also persuaded him that if he sold his ranch to Alf Whiting for sixty thousand dollars, he would have a nest egg he could legally bring out in the open that would keep him in dignity for the rest of his natural life."

"Dignity, yes," said Taorelli. "I'm sure you had something to do with his reconciliation with his wife, my cousin."

"To an extent," said Hewitt. "When I talked to her, I found that she was still in love with the little bastard. Love is something I can't account for, but there it was. And Hethcutt wanted her back so badly that he was willing to put the entire amount—one hundred and thirty-five thousand—in her name and under her control."

Gabrielini sighed. "Ah, yes. I heard just today that they will live in Fiorenza, Italy—Florence, to you. One can live very handsomely there on the income from that much money, without ever touching the principal. I feel very humble—and very grateful to you, gentlemen—when I realize how close he came to making good his drunken brag of becoming a millionaire. And he will still live a life of luxury!"

"I believe that is the case," Hewitt said. "Alf Whiting will be quite comfortable on a rather valuable cattle property, too. Doesn't it make you feel good to know you have regained your money, and at the same time brought so much happiness to people?"

A waiter brought the next course—veal in a sauce that Gabrielini recommended highly—and a new wine to go with it. He opened the bottle and offered Gabrielini the ritual first sip. The banker nodded his approval and waited until the waiter had served the others and departed.

"Do you realize," he said, "that you have made it possible for two thieves to get away with enough of their loot to live happily ever after?"

"Yes," said Hewitt, "but you are our client, and they're your thieves, married into your families." He shook his finger reprovingly at the banker. "You have condoned for years a traffic in opium for another family combine, Lon Tsan's—one that resulted in the addiction and death of an innocent puma. I regard that as a crime against nature, personally."

"Family!" Gabrielini sighed. "It is a great comfort, but it can be a burden, too."

"I wouldn't know. I have no family," said Hewitt.

"Which reminds me," said Nick Taorelli. "My first cousin once removed, Bella Whiting, told me today that she had written you a note, asking you to have supper with her tomorrow at this very restaurant, and that you have not replied."

"Please be so kind as to carry my reply to her, and make my apologies. I am catching a train eastward with Conrad tomorrow morning at six-thirty."

Gabrielini and Taorelli looked at Conrad, who nodded confirmation. The banker looked back at Hewitt.

"You would become a member of a powerful, closely knit, loyal family if you married Bella," he said. "After all, she's a Taorelli as well as a Whiting."

"But a family is the one thing I can't afford," Hewitt said. "In my job, you have to be a loner."